Cover art:
Courtesy of Costa Rican artist David Artavia.
His wonderful paintings reflect a love of nature that is evident in every detail.
artavia.araya@gmail.com
Instagram: @davidartaviaart_
Facebook: David Artavia Art Gallery

Lola Pereira Varela

The Souls of Cabo Blanco

Translated from Spanish

by Gianfranco Gómez Zamora

Las almas de Cabo Blanco
Printed and published: BoD - Books on Demand, Norderstedt
ISBN: 9783756224364
Printed in Germany
© Lola Pereira Varela, 2022
Revised edition of: Mensajeros del Futuro, EUNED 2018, with new title.
The Souls of Cabo Blanco
English translation: Gianfranco Gómez Zamora
Cover design: Martina Wegener and Gianfranco Gómez Zamora
Photographs courtesy of Patricia Slump

To all my students

At the Liceo Rural Santa Teresa

To Álvaro Ugalde,

Who gifted me his affection and dedication.

…although he is no longer among us,

I know his splendor illuminates,

like the stars from above…

If all insects disappeared, all life on earth would perish.

If all humans disappeared, all life on earth would flourish.

Jonas Salk 1914-1995

Karen and Nicolás in Costa Rica, 1955

Prologue

Karen Mogensen and Nils Olof Wessberg came to Costa Rica from Sweden in 1955 to live in harmony with nature. They soon realized that the Costa Ricans did not treat the plants and animals in a way that they considered appropriate. They had an interventionist attitude, which initially received little approval from the residents. But Karen and Olof persevered and in 1963 they managed to establish a nature reserve in Cabo Blanco, the first in Costa Rica. Their tireless efforts to protect nature ended in tragedy, however.

Nils Olof Wessberg was assassinated on July 23, 1975 while preparing a species inventory in the Rain Forest of Corcovado, Osa Peninsula, and thus becoming the first martyr of the conservation struggle in this country. With their work and sacrifice, Doña Karen and Don Nicolás, as the locals called Karen and Nils Olof, have become "The Souls of Cabo Blanco" who protect the forest and its animals for all eternity.

Lola Pereira Varela tells the story in the form of a diary written by Karen. Her tender feelings for wildlife, as well as the affectionate description of the trees and the ocean are depicted in the story. Costa Rican rural life spanning from the nineteen-fifties to the nineteen-nineties is impressively portrayed with all its joy, but also with its uncertainty. This book preserves the memory and dedication of the founders of the first nature reserve in Costa

Rica. Their influence on the conservation movement is unprecedented and it is difficult to speculate what would have become of the natural areas without their urgent intervention to stop the destruction of the forest and all the life it contains. Today a third of the country is protected and Costa Rica is world renowned for its brand of ecotourism.

It is important to clarify that some of the characters and entities mentioned in this story are fictitious to a certain extent and that real names were changed when it was considered prudent to do so. The publisher is exempt from any responsibility for the veracity of the facts contained in the story.

PART ONE

Karen waiting for Nicolas at their house in Cocalito.

Harrowing dreams

Early morning of July 23rd, 1975.

*T*he monotonous buzz of the cicadas, the repeated, ominous litany and unvarying rhythm of the notes, carried a somnolence that prevented my eyes from opening. My eyelids were heavy, as if a mountain of earth laid on top of each of them. I tried to discern the figure approaching amid the torrential rain. Startled, I recognized it was you, but there was something strange in your step, which usually had a paused, long stride. You stumbled closer and I saw your pallid face, ashen, soaked with rain. I asked if you liked what you had seen in Corcovado and you answered no; it is always cold in Punta Llorona, you said shivering, your voice as thin as a thread.

You covered yourself from the rain with your military coat, the one you used in Sweden when you were a captain in the air force. The blue and yellow national emblem, with its three crowns, stood out from the khaki green. I was confused, however, because except for your knife and rucksack, we had not brought any of your military gear. As you approached, the path behind you vanished, as if dissolving in the torrential rain...

I awoke suddenly, startled by the urgent cries of the roosters from the Cruz family farm, our nearest neighbors. It seemed impossible to hear them from so far away, but I know that sound travels differently at night. It was three in the morning. I rose from bed with a hasty impulse, shivering. I listened to the echo of the night and drank some water so I could feel the dense liquid flow down my throat and dispel the unease provoked by the nightmare. I had to make sure that I had left the dream. Even so, I asked you with a desperate scream that I did not wish to stifle: Where are you? What has happened, that you have not returned?....

I went out to the corridor. Little by little, the dragging murmur of the waves on the sand, like a tongue of white foam in the midst of darkness, calmed my anguish. Nevertheless, I could no longer sleep. The night became eternal, until the sun rose from behind the mountain and awakened the day.

It was a hot, humid, sticky day. By the end of the afternoon, I had finished making the buttonholes and attaching the buttons on the sixth and final shirt. I wandered idly on Playa Colorada, counting the pelicans as they flew in their V-formation, their constellation stretching and fluctuating, and they provoked my envy once more. I was moved by their capacity to travel the world and return where they started, detached from everything and everyone. I observe these magical beings daily, autonomous and free. I think they must have their own, independent feelings and emotions. They live independently and raise their young without human arrogance. They live on the cliff as it were an impenetrable castle, their own watchtower. Maybe one day, in another galaxy, I too will be able to fly…

I recalled a lovely Bereber legend, from Morocco, in Africa. Years ago, I read in a travel magazine about a plaza in Marrakech named Jemaa el Fna. The roofs of all the surrounding houses are adorned with prickly, round stork nests; those elegant migratory birds, with white, black-tipped feathers, which I always envied in Denmark. The Bereber legend claims they are the residents of the plaza, that feel the call of adventure and the urge to know new horizons. They then turn into storks and fly off to see the world, returning to their home once they have achieved their goal.

How I wish I could do this. As a girl I dreamt so many times that I could fly, contemplating the world from above. I don't know how these images registered in my mind, but I have detailed memories of the church towers, with their pointy belfries. I could see the green from the blades of grass, delineating the silhouettes of tiny purple flowers, growing between the tiles and in cracks on the rooftops.

Maybe I was also a bird in another life. If I had a choice, I would have been a hummingbird, with brilliantly green feathers; a White-necked Jacobin, *Florisuga mellivora*, with a scaly breast, buzzing from one heliconia to the next, in search of that marvelous nectar. I would roam the forest, living gratefully among the trees. If I were a denizen of the forest, I would live in strangler fig. It would be a magnificent, cozy home, with its mushroom shape, its brilliant leaves, and its lianas, which resemble the fringes of a beautiful, aerial dress. The perfect shelter.

The stroll calmed my restless spirit and I returned to the house as the sun hid on the horizon, hoping I would find you there. Neither you nor the boat had arrived, but as I bathed, I was filled with the illusion that you would be home for dinner and that we would share our bed that night and the caresses which we had treasured during your leave.

It was almost dark when I heard the motor of the boat approaching and I ran to the beach. All I saw when I arrived was a wake of white foam, drawn upon the iridescent skin of the Pacific. When the ocean was rough, the boat would land in front of our house, on the calm Playa Colorada, as the waters there are more still than at Montezuma, where the impetuous waves coil and crash on the sand. But today this was not necessary; as the waves lazily dragged the sand, moving it up and down, like a slow, measured waltz. I waited for you on the road that goes to Montezuma while there was still a splash of sun on the ocean. The gray clouds dyed to an intense crimson, preparing for the evening. The ocean shifted, cradling the volcanic rocks, leaving watermarks of white foam over their dark mass. I watched from the high part of the road, sensing the privilege of belonging to this place. It is such a beautiful place....

Little by little, the night acquired more darkness, extinguishing the brilliance of the orange sun. The moon arrived, almost full, white, and cold, penciling a path of burnished silver over the ocean, titillating, and leaping over the skin of the water. I waited in vain for you to arrive. I returned to the house frustrated and went to bed, fearing a replica of the dream from the night before. Despite my apprehension, exhaustion overtook me.

July 27

The irritating and repetitive ring-ring of the telephone sounded threatening. Someone yelled "Olof is on the phone!" I ran barefoot towards the door, feeling the knots of the wooden floor under my feet, and looked for the telephone on the corridor table. I could barely lift the heavy receiver, jet black, brilliant, and articulated, like a giant beetle. I told you how much I missed you, bursting with emotion. I recounted that a new coati had arrived at the house injured and that life without you wasn't worth much, even in paradise. I asked when you would be returning but could not understand your response. I yelled into the phone, telling you that it was nearly my birthday and you had promised to be back home so we could celebrate together. I screamed louder, forcing my throat to ask: "Where are you?".... but your voice was fading, as if it were being swallowed by a drain into the earth. I awoke from the pain in my throat brought on by my own screams, my breathing altered and the sheets tangled around my withered body, damaged by your absence…

We did not have a telephone in Cocalito. There were no telephones in Montezuma or in Corcovado. It was impossible to hear a telephone ringing or to speak to you. My subconscious was telling me something, but I could not decipher the message. Perhaps it was denial, a resistance to what my intuition already knew: something was not right.

As time passes, I have come to repent immensely not having accompanied you on that trip. I felt tired from an entire week of cutting and sewing your long-sleeve shirts, so you could ward off Corcovado's abundant mosquitoes. We could never find that type of shirt in the stores, because of your height, which is not common here. But you did not want to wait, you were rushing to find a place to settle down and begin the inventory. Now there is no use in crying over spilled milk, as the old adage says.

I threw a resentful glare at the pile of folded shirts, tailored in olive green, your favorite color. There were six, one on top of another, resting on the dresser and waiting to be worn for the first time. I buried my face in them, breathing deeply, searching uselessly for your scent, and I sat cross-legged in the *padmasana* position to meditate. My hands were clasped in prayer. I had to calm my troubled spirit. Shaken, I searched for my inner guide and prayed that my restless soul find peace.

The sound of the vibration of the universe, ommmmm… escaped my lips undulating slightly, caressing the back of my throat. It continued its exodus, merging with the cries of the Mantled Howler monkeys which travelled the air, potent and vibrant, from the old pochote tree. It floated over the umbrellalike orange-green leaves of the beach almonds, shaken by the sea breeze blowing from Playa Colorada, and continued its wandering journey towards the mountains.

I tried breathing deeply and alternatively in *Anuloma Vilona,* then concentrating on *Suryanamascar,* the salute to the sun. Unlike other days, I finished my routine and calm eluded me. I told myself that neither body nor spirit can remain steady every day.

It was a strange day; the coatis and squirrels were constantly in and out of the house. Their head movements, looking from one side to the other, reminded me of spectators at a tennis match and made me laugh. I am certain they looked for you, especially *Lis*, the coati, who had adopted us as her family. When she didn't find you, she retraced her movements in an established ritual, returning to the usual places, again and again. Then they looked at me, as if interrogating me, and went back outside. They were the best companions to my fallen spirit.

I went to bed without dinner. I was not hungry or sleepy. Exhaustion brought on by frustration and fear left me without support, like a rag doll. The fear of fear. The fear of thinking about the meaning of your absence.

I search for you

August 5th

*Y*ou walked towards me on a dirt path, shaded by trees. A dense drizzle fell, mixed with shreds of gray fog which crawled slowly from the trees to the dirt floor. I opened the door and was enveloped by the fog. I peeked out to the corridor; you were approaching, offering a branch of red hibiscus with your large, elegant hands. You held it in your left hand, gently folded, and tenderly handed it to me. You bestowed it in my hands softly, as if entrusting me with a divine creature, a legacy to save the world. Your gaze escaped your sunken eye sockets, darkened by fatigue. I had seen you like this before, exhausted by the construction of the house. I now noticed your despair, your infinite sorrow, so thick it was palpable…

Dawn rose cold and gray and I awoke shaken, at that moment when night ceases to be but it is not yet day. Yesterday was August 4th, my birthday. Through the window I watched the clouds conglomerate in the sky as the air dragged them toward the hills, threatening rain. I removed the sheets and put my feet on the floor, feeling diminished, without enough strength to draw breath and enclosed by ominous thoughts. It was so strange having a birthday without you. You know ever since I can remember, throughout my life, my dreams have revealed premonitions. This is the reason I can't be calm. There is something I can't understand, or perhaps I resist understanding.

I lit our two candles, together, an unusual gesture, as daylight neared, but something drove me to do it. I peeked out to the corridor to feel the sea breeze on my face, but I was startled when I turned and saw that your candle had blown out, while mine was still shining. I interpreted it as a fateful omen. Everything has a meaning, a purpose. Nothing happens by chance. Coincidences do not exist, of this I am certain.

These messages, directed only towards me, were disturbing. I could no longer stand the uncertainty and I left for Puntarenas, 15 days after your departure. So, we are off, me and my soul, cramped into this small aircraft, its doors tethered by ropes, at the mercy of the winds and at the pleasure of destiny…

I departed for Cóbano yesterday morning, as soon as I could find Edwin, that young man with the beaten-up Toyota. I wished I was invisible, while travelling on the muddy, pothole infested road leading to the small aircraft, so that no one could ask me where I was going or why. I don't want to be a social animal today, one that needs interaction with other human beings.

We stealthily crossed the town intersection. The people of Cóbano, busy with their daily chores, seemed surreal, as if suspended in midair, like images in a vintage photograph. My thoughts were consumed by you, there was no space for anything else. Your existence was my only desire. I was lethargic, in a hypnotic state, and everything around me seemed surreal.

I called our usual hotel in San José from the checkpoint at the airstrip before boarding the plane, in case you were in the city purchasing the tents we would need for our planned the trip together. They informed me you were not there, although they had been expecting you for a few days now.

I wobbly climbed the steps into the plane that brought me from Cóbano to Puntarenas. The pilot offered me his arm for support, asking if I was not well. I was unable to answer. I don't know if I am well or unwell. I saw him glance at me, from the corner of his eye, as he started the motors of the toy-like aircraft. The propeller began to spin and the toy slid down the dirt runway, lifting up and heading west, towards an area devoid of vegetation. The ocean appeared instantly and we bordered the coast at low altitude, somewhere between the blue sky and the green Pacific. The plane's shadow resembled a miniscule sardine, floating in the intensely blue air.

The trip lasted fifteen eternal minutes, beset by uncertainty. I felt within me the interruption of the connective thread. That thread that we both know so well; that synchrony which allows us to imagine the same thing at the same instant and which permanently intensifies our union.

I could not imagine, no matter how long I closed my eyes, what you might be doing. I could not visualize what you might be observing. A thick fog covered my eyes. Only the images from my dreams returned again and again, leaving me weakened, defenseless, draining me of life.

I consoled myself thinking that the passing of time was in my favor; that at this time tomorrow things would be different because I would have found you. I tried to tell myself that it was only a matter of time and Cronos, in this case, was my ally.

Years ago, we would talk about the worst thing that could happen when travelling in small aircrafts. Hypothetically, if the plane should go down, we would look at each other serenely, accepting destiny, as a tribute to the life we had chosen. I could not think about that now, perhaps because the possibility of tragedy seemed closer now than we had ever imagined. Also, whichever tragedy might occur, it would be in the singular, while you and I are still one unit and whatever happens, good or bad, is communal.

Upon landing, we bumped along the Chacarita airstrip, feeling the rough terrain through the wheels of the craft. I hurriedly jumped into the only taxi there and asked him to take me to the port so I could inquire about you. As we approached the pier where the boat to Punta Llorona was moored, the scent of burnt petroleum filled my lungs, and brought on a nausea I could barely contain. The odor, potent and disgusting, was augmented by my hypersensitive state of mind, which turned me into a delicate flower, newly opened to the world. I thought about the rose in *The Little Prince* and its glass dome. Like her, I needed a glass dome to protect me from adversities that threatened my mental and physical integrity.

I approached the edge of the water and asked one of the mariners if he had seen you return from Punta Llorona, as he adjusted a new flag to the mast of the boat. He answered with contempt that because of low demand, the boat schedules had changed and "now we make that trip every 15 days." The trip was scheduled for the following week.

Finally, my chest expanded, breaking the shell of fear, and I could breathe deeply once more. I concluded that you could not return because there was no boat, and you had no way of letting me know. I had to contain myself to keep from jumping for joy...sometimes the smallest things are so satisfying. Despite my relief, something seemed off. I could not reestablish our inner symbiosis...nor imagine you, nor recreate you in any point in the universe. You existed only in my nighttime dreams.

I decided to dispel my senseless misgivings and make the most of the trip before returning home. I walked to the market in Puntarenas to purchase items I could not find in Montezuma. The asphalt burned and I hid from the scorching afternoon sun as I walked. I made my way through the chiaroscuro of the store corridors, with relief fluttering in my head, but without a perch to rest on.

I was entering the supermarket, when a young girl with a graceful face called out to me as she crossed the dusty street, looking at me kindly. She lowered her turquoise umbrella, clasping a little boy by the hand, and asked I had found my husband, with a troubled expression reflected in her chestnut brown eyes. Bewildered, I shot back: "And how do you know I am looking for my husband?"

I wanted to imagine that it was just the nightmares assaulting me again, as she assured me that an article with your photograph had appeared in the newspaper *La Nación* two days earlier, stating you were irretrievably lost in the wilderness of Punta Llorona. Clinging to a different reality, I told her the article was not about you, that it was about a couple of foreigners who had disappeared near Puerto Jiménez a few days ago and still had not turned up. Camilo, from the pulperia, had shown me the newspaper article. But she insisted that the newspaper mentioned don Nicolas, "the Swede of the horses", as you are known by everyone. My heart skipped and I brought my hand to my chest, to prevent my heart from bursting out of my body.

I rushed to the Pérez family home, in Puntarenas. Alejandro, Oliver, and their mother welcomed me affectionately. They tried to reassure me, cheerfully and patiently, as they brewed coffee and heated up tortillas with soft cheese. They pointed out what I had already imagined about your absence. It was all very clear to them: you were reveling, ecstatic, contemplating the forest and oblivious to the rest of world, as always. They were sure that nothing had happened, because you were an intelligent, capable man, like no other…but they could not convince me.

They were more concerned about the squatter invasion in Curú. The inspectors from the Land and Colonization Institute had arrived with the plans drawn to distribute land. They told me that Henry, a trusted employee, had stayed behind to safeguard the property. Apparently, eighty families from San Ramón had arrived, almost three-hundred people in all, to appropriate the land.

It was unclear how it would all play out, but they were very worried because President Oduber had promised land to landless farmers during the election. Now that he had won, he had to keep his promise and would adjudicate titled properties to the squatters.

To them it was an injustice, because they had paid for the land and taken care of it all these years. They were also afraid it would result in mass deforestation, to make way for cattle pastures and rice and beans plantations. Without a doubt, all life in the forest would suffer, they lamented. Internally I was burning with desire to rush out the door and find the airplane pilot, but I listened courteously to their considerations, because they had always treated us with such affection.

As soon as I could, I left in search of the pilot to fly to Corcovado. I could not wait any longer, inside I knew that too much time was already lost. I searched each and every house in El Roble, asking for Gerardo the pilot. I finally found him at ten o'clock at night, in a little house with an aqua green fence and a corridor packed with plants and cats of every size and color. I knew it was not a proper hour to call on a decent household, since life in the country takes place in the daylight and nighttime is for sleeping. And this town is still rural, even though it is changing. Gerardo was sleeping soundly in his bedroom. He came to the door with his hair tangled and stern face. He asked in a single sentence and with a gruff voice what was so urgent and how he could help. I apologized and spoke to him of your disappearance. In the same, sleepy voice he explained he had several previously scheduled flights for the next morning; but my desperation was evident, and he took pity on me. We arranged a departure time for the next day.

I went to Pensión Cabezas in an attempt to get some rest. I booked the same room that we get when we travel together. They asked about you, puzzled by your absence, but as it was late, and I did not want to explain. My voice would not manifest itself outwardly. I simply told them I was on my way to find you, because that was the truth.

I have been writing nearly all through the night. I can't tell if I have slept in bits, exhausted from writing in my tense state. I feel like I have slept with my eyes open, they are so irritated. I don't recall if I dreamt or how many times I tossed and turned. The disheveled sheets are the only witnesses of this tormented night.

August 6th

We departed from the Chacarita airstrip at five in the morning and Gerardo complained that he had not gotten enough sleep. Although I apologized for waking him, my apology was insincere, because I would have done it again. The taxi to the airstrip took me past the Pérez home. Although their front door was open, I did not stop to greet them. They did not know about my trip to Punta Llorona. The meteorology office warned of gusting winds, but I refused to listen. Even the chirping birds, always lovely and pleasing, brought on a dismal foreboding that clipped my breath. They sang ceaselessly, all night long. Perhaps they were just accompanying me, nature is so intuitive and soothing…

The aircraft flies parallel to the cemetery at lift off and my gaze sweeps the white tombs, once adorned with flourishing floral crowns, but now offensively colored in decay, imbued with fuchsia, red, and orange. They look rusted, the flowers indistinct from the leaves, the crucifixes, or the faded dedications of "YOU ARE NOT FORGOTTEN" written on purple ribbons. The scene rehashes an old and arbitrary tone; that time is the ultimate leveler, because in time everything is forgotten.

Where are you?

I look away from the graves, lined with walkways, and a chill sweeps my spine, from my coccyx to the top of my head. It is not a fear of flying; I cannot define the quiver I felt. The sun shines over the vibrant blue and flashes on the windows, forcing me to close my eyes.

I am on my way to search for you, my love. I will find you, wherever you are, because I will not stop until I do. At that moment, as I travel from point to point, from Puntarenas to Punta Llorona, bordering the coast in a small and minimal aircraft, at the mercy of the swirling wind, I sort through my perceptions of the past few days. I try to organize my ideas, which are laid out in this notebook, tattered and worn from flipping the pages over and over, trying to find the reason for your absence in my written words.

It has been fifteen days since you left on your expedition, looking for a place for us to live while conducting the species inventory in Corcovado. "At least six months", you said we would need, and I began making a list of essential supplies, preparing to relocate there from our home in Cocalito.

You agreed to return for my birthday. The day before yesterday I turned forty-nine, alone, because you did not return. Never, since the day we met, had we been apart on August 4th…the gusts of wind shake the aircraft like a dried leaf, causing my hand to convulse, writing illegibly, and smudging my notebook. I hope I don't need to revisit my notes.

I fill the lined pages in this notebook since yesterday, writing everything down so that nothing is lost, nothing is forgotten. All the while, I know you will laugh when we read it together at what you call my "female capacity." "From a grain of sand, you are capable of making mountain the size of Sweden's Mount Kebnekaise", and once again you will burst out in laughter, which will reverberate off the white walls of our home. And I will turn my back on you, pretending to be upset, as you sometimes do.

Some of our neighbors think you are always angry because most days that is the side you show them. They do not understand that you anger stems from their destructive behavior towards wildlife, even domestic animals and pets. Especially horses, those affectionate, intelligent, and noble beings, that they abuse relentlessly, until their death…

I explore my theory about the passage of time and our perception of its flexibility as rational beings. During good times, time flows with the speed of water sliding off a mountain cliff, advancing unconsciously, stone by stone, like young deer fawn leaping through the thick of the forest. And so, without realizing it, minute by minute, the days and weeks flow in what seems like an ephemeral instant.

On the other hand, when awaiting the birth of a child, or a special event, it seems like the clock is delayed. Every instant is carried individually in the opposite direction by miniature gnomes; upriver, from the lowlands to the mountain, their toddler feet crashing on every crack on the path. Although sometimes, when there is a passing ailment or when a wound is healing, the passage of time, albeit slow, is in our favor. As the grains of sand in the hourglass slide from one crystal cavity to the other, our health and wellbeing recover.

For this to come to fruition, it is indispensable to have hope, an essential ingredient in the composition of the balm that heals our wounds.

The trouble is when the time we are allotted is not enough to reach the place where we are awaited. When the distance grows with every step, and reaching our destination becomes impossible, like those dreams in which we walk and walk, but never reach our destination, eventually forgetting our course.

I have always believed that time is the most precious thing we have. When someone is kind enough to offer their time, they offer us their greatest value, because our life here is accounted for down the very last second. We are so unaware that we are only passing by.

I search my memory for the Emily Dickinson poem about hope, to which I cling so I can find you.

"Hope" is the thing with feathers -

That perches in the soul -

And sings the tune without the words -

And never stops - at all -

And sweetest - in the Gale - is heard -

And sore must be the storm -

That could abash the little Bird

That kept so many warm -

I've heard it in the chillest land -

And on the strangest Sea -

Yet - never - in Extremity,

It asked a crumb - of me.

I want to think that in this moment, as I go to you, time is on my side; because with every advance, with every averted vortex, we are closer to finding each other again.

I rest my notebook on the seat beside me, searching for a solid surface on which to write and for an eternal moment I close my eyes as I continue writing. I blink, as I look out the window, trying to stave the irritation on my eyes caused by the dazzling sun on the cloudless sky.

A high-pressure system has arrived and the celestial sphere is an intense, deep blue today. I had to work hard to convince the pilot, in addition to paying him charter rate, even though it was only him and I on the plane, no one else. You would always say: "Money is never better spent than when it serves a good purpose." This cause is more than any other: finding you in that mountainous wilderness is the most important thing today.

I feel afflicted and fatigued by my repeated, and failed efforts to feel your vital pulse, as I breathe deeply, consuming my faltering energy. Returning again and again to my memories of the last few days…

I open my eyes and blink, observing the beauty of the coastal landscape. Not even my pain can ignore the unspoiled beauty before my eyes. The coast, so neatly cut, covered in vegetation illustrated by the trees, marks the limit between land and sea. The solidity of the rock and the fluidity of the water in a constant dispute, without respite.

I see the peninsula of Manuel Antonio, jutting into the Pacific and forming its horseshoe shaped bays; one bigger, the other smaller. Further down, rivaling its beauty, Punta Ballena, reflecting the tail of an enormous cetacean, shaking the waves, its body anchored to the continent. I feel so small up here, stunned by the perfection of this prodigious ecosystem. Without a doubt, such beauty had to be the work of many different beings. If it were the work on one being then it must be a magnificent and omnipotent entity.

I stop writing as the landing wheels drag the sand on the beach, tracing two parallel lines. I hope I will not have to come back to this notebook, because I will find you here, inside this beachside ranch with a palm thatched roof, onto which my hope fearfully clings.

Finally, after nearly an hour of bordering the coastline, soaked in beauty and penitence, we landed on the dry sand of the beach. We observed the tide and concluded that our stop must be brief, as the high tide was already filling in. I paid the pilot and asked him to wait a moment, so we could depart immediately in case you were there. He left the plane to stretch his legs and walked along the water's edge slowly, waiting for my return.

I hurriedly jumped from the plane and noticed something was off, as the arrival of a plane was always a joyful occasion and the children would surround it, hoping for a candy handout. I had been there on my own a few months back, when you had hurt your foot and could not walk. On that occasion I met that nice young man, Fernando Vargas, who took me to the forest in search of avocado seeds. The boy, who was just an adolescent, had told me they were not in season, but I asked him to accompany me all the same and what I saw astounded me. It shocked me in such a way as only the beauty of nature, unaltered by the deviance of man, can do. At sunset, large groups of Scarlet Macaws hovered over a giant Guanacaste Tree, like beautiful, fatuous streaks of fire suspended in midair. At that moment, I understood the Stendhal syndrome, inducing paroxysm in the presence of beauty.

It was the most beautiful primary forest I could ever imagine. That is how I described it to you and it was the motive for your trip there. On this occasion, it was I who could not go, but you did not want to wait any longer. You felt an urgency to witness the beauty I had described. The excitement sparkled in your eyes and kept you on edge, like a little boy about to open a gift. You could no longer bear to wait and you had always been hesitant to change any laid out plans. You had learned in the military to follow through with the plans ordered by your superiors, and that had not changed. Once you had decided that something had to be done in a certain way, you would not change course, and I knew that.

Everything was still and silent in Llorona, not even the chickens stirred. I walked towards the ranches and entered the first one I came to. Two boys were sitting in there, so saddened, they barely mustered a "Good morning."

Something terrible had happened, it was plain to see in their troubled faces and fleeting gazes. My anguish increased gradually. I asked sternly about my husband, but they said they had no news. A young woman and the two boys replied in unison that they had not seen him since he left the camp a few days ago.

The woman said they thought it strange he had not returned and they had notified the police at the post in Puerto Jiménez. I understood, at that moment, how the report had made it into the newspapers. Despite the report, the police had not shown up to look for you. I imagined that nobody searched for the missing if a relative did not file a report, as if not having family somehow voided your existence.

I told the airplane pilot he could leave and walked back to the ranch, where the woman was brewing coffee through a strainer into an aluminum pitcher, covered in dents and blacked from daily use. I asked about your belongings and they directed me to the ranch next door. There, resting on a wooden plank of almendro, was your diary with notes and sketches you had made as you travelled by boat to Llorona. I snatched it up, as if it were a map that could lead me to you. I saw your written words, a bit distorted, but clean and clear. As I looked at the trees, their leaves and branches drawn with long lines, I could almost see you working, labeling each tree with its respective name. I knew the way your hands had moved to trace those lines. You always started with an outline of aerial lines and filled in with shadows afterwards.

Your handwriting was small and unsteady. Ever since you had your lateral paralysis, you wrote using only two fingers on your left hand. You named each and every tree species and that shook me. We had never corresponded. From the moment we met, we had not been separated long enough to justify correspondence.

I kept flipping pages and I found a sketch of a tapir with her calf. I envisioned you drawing them filled with tenderness and wholly content, as you drew that snout, edged in white, and the irregular horizontal lines on its back. They were laying down at rest, facing each other, and I tingled as I imagined your ecstasy. You adore these huge, peaceful animals. It was one of the reasons you had come to Corcovado. They had been exterminated in Cabo Blanco before we arrived and we had never see them. After we created the reserve, twelve years ago, we had hoped they would someday return, but it was not so. I understood that your diary was a message directed towards me and that brought me momentary serenity, as if it validated your existence. Your diary assured me that I had not imagined you. You really did exist, and I was going to find you.

I decided quickly to look for local guides among the people drinking coffee with tortillas in the ranch. In a loud voice, I offered a hefty reward to anyone that would accompany in an exploration into the forest. Two young men and a middle-aged man stepped up and stood beside me. The older man had a certain mysticism in the way he spoke, invoking God every other word: "if God permits", or "God willing." Together, we set off into the forest with a steady step.

I looked into the treetops and the vegetation all around us, allowing my intuition to guide us. I thought to myself: what you would do? I attempted to make a mental connection with you, but the line was broken. I could not feel your pulse beating on any frequency. I unleashed one last cry from my most intimate innerself, searching in vain for a signal of your response.

I led the group as I imagined you at the foot of the trees, whose trunks were thick with lianas, while birds noisily chased each other in the game of life. It was a primary forest and you could walk easily on the forest floor, which was completely free of undergrowth. The sun attempted fruitlessly to penetrate the tangle of lianas, which held giant garlands of vines from the trees; wrapped with rounded, lilac ipomeas. We walked through patches of sun and shade, like patches of light in a painting by Pierre-Auguste Renoir. My instinct took me on a path that I was certain you had walked. I looked around, like a dog sniffing out its prey, searching for any signal, a track or a scent, that would attest to your presence. I listened to the raucous call of the cicadas and the wheezing anxiety that squeezed my lungs. My parched throat began to sting. We had walked more than 30 minutes and had found no signals that would lead us to you.

I was visually exploring the landscape, as if my eyes were a camera on alert, trying to discover any object out of place that would instantly reveal your image. It was not long before I discovered a knife, stabbed with fury into a wild cashew tree. It was not a gesture that would come naturally to you. "There!", I yelled, and stood paralyzed and in alert.

I stopped breathing for a moment, so I could concentrate on your sudden appearance. I stood at the foot of the wild cashew tree with the middle-aged man who examined the knife thoroughly, without touching it. I sent the young men each in a different direction and I stood watchful, waiting.

The sound of gurgling water rose from a nearby creek and I wanted to imagine that you had gone down there for a drink; that you would appear suddenly and scold me for my absurd anxiety. On this occasion I would not mind the reprimand. My thoughts came and went, fluttering through my head like an agitated flock of birds.

It was August 6th; the continued nightmares had weakened me due to lack of sleep and my appetite diminished so I was barely eating. I felt a pinch in my belly and I looked at my waist. I saw my wrinkled white shirt, suffering the two days of travel. My pant hems were covered in mud. I was irritated that I had neglected myself, I did not like the thought that you would see me like this. I tried to straighten out the wrinkles in my shirt and fix my hair behind my ears, so that when you showed up you wouldn't see me in such a disastrous state. I wet my lips and practiced a smile for you, feeling somewhat ridiculous.

As I waited I thought about the day we met, at the Raw Food Guest House in Humlegården. I thought you were the most handsome man I had ever met. I concluded in that instant, suddenly finding myself in love, that I wanted to live with you forever. Now I was gripped by doubt, how long is "forever"?

Reminiscing

Denmark 1952

I remember the first day we met. You were dishing salad made of raw red cabbage, radishes, and carrots into those white plates adorned with a green flower on the edge that they used in the Humlegården Raw Food Guesthouse. Back then I was twenty-six and you were thirty-three. You were so handsome, so tall, you stood out from all the rest. You were wearing your Swedish Air Force uniform and initially I couldn't tell if you were real or a dream. Later, while we dined facing each other, I could see the most beautiful landscapes in the world, the deep oceans, the mountains full of life with the rivers gurgling down their slopes and all the constellations of the universe through your clean and kind gaze. I never wanted to be separated from you. You were my world, my only port of call, in calm waters and during the storms. That connection was our strongest bond, our vital pulse forever.

You heard about Dr. Kristine Nolfi's nutritional therapies to combat cancer while you were consigned to the military detachment in Skövde. I worked at that center because I wanted to closely observe the effects of treatment on the patients, due to my diagnosis of myxedema. Although there were many people who dined with us that night, my eyes saw only you.

I sort through my memories, one by one, as if I were breaking grains off a tender corn husk. We both rejected a model of life sustained by a shameless waste of resources and by polluting the air, water, and land with agrochemicals; aware that the development of any civilization always leads to catastrophe because that is the only way that human beings reproduce. We both shared the belief that the agrochemicals used in food production were the cause of many diseases, including cancer.

I remember sadly your first attempt at a self-sufficient organic garden in Speleby, with the idea of creating the Commune of Friends of Speleby. It became an impossible task, despite your efforts, due to the terrible frosts and low temperatures which made growth and maturation difficult. There was not enough sun for any fruit trees to produce sweet, juicy fruit. The cold reigned most of the year and there was no way to protect the trees from the harsh winter. You tried for seven years. I helped you the last two, but the difficulties overcame us.

During those two years we suffered the hardship of surviving on raw vegetarian food in a harsh winter climate. Our diet consisted of vegetables, sprouted grains, apples, and milk. We didn't even eat cooked potatoes or cheese, bread, or butter. After two years on this diet, even the sweetest apples were bitter on our palates, and we were desperate because we couldn't satisfy our need to eat the way we wanted.

Fighting against the weather is an illusory task. The fight is always titanic and defeat is guaranteed. The cold forces us to heat our homes until mid-June and causes the trees to turn bare when they lose their leaves in August. The trees know, as I do, that although the calendar says that there are three months of summer in Sweden, there are really only two. The rest is desolation. We were convinced that some other life, with less effort and less expenditure of resources, was possible somewhere in the world.

We read Son Waerland, who was considered a health philosopher in Sweden. He wrote about the causes of diseases. Cancer was one of them, and he agreed with Dr. Nolfi on the benefits of raw vegetables and the destruction of nutrients when cooked with fire. Yes, even then you had declared war on fire, on all the fires.

We learned from our research that a great variety of fruits were produced in Central America which made it possible to eat adequately. That was what encouraged our decision to emigrate in 1954.

For a year and a half we explored Ecuador, Panama, Nicaragua, Honduras, El Salvador, Guatemala, Mexico and Costa Rica; in search of fruit. It was in vain. There was not a single place where a fruit orchard had been planted. Only scattered trees, born at random.

We required at least ten different types of fruit to sustain us throughout the year, due to their seasonal nature. We learned of the enormous task we would have to overcome in order to feed ourselves. Today, fruit is diverse and abundant and sold everywhere. This seems natural to us now, but it was not so back then.

The love for animals and nature came later, when we were already installed in Cocalito. When the wild, orphaned sons and daughters of the forest came to our house, seeking protection. Their mothers had been killed and their habitats destroyed. But that happened over time. When our house was built, we were able to take care of the animals that were given to us or that came looking for the shelter of our home.

At the time we decided to leave Europe we wanted to escape our genetics and a probable death from cancer. Also, we did not want to live according to the European model. Countries full of people who only had enough time to work, day after day and with no hope of change. Civilization is destructive. Fairfield Osborn's book *Our Plundered Planet* was our bible, in which we read the author's arguments about the multiplication of the human species and the inadequacy of the earth's resources to feed them. That worried us and it is still something to be resolved, since consumerism has worsened the model of life since the book was published in 1948. Now all people want an easy life and they have engines that work for them and everything is possible with minimal effort, but this is unsustainable for the planet. The next generations will suffer the consequences of our waste. We are squandering the gift of life on this planet, our common home.

Aboard the *Astrid Bakke*

*T*here are so many images of you in my head. On February 13, 1954, on the cargo ship *Astrid Bakke* as we left the seaport of Stockholm for Ecuador. We watched as families waved goodbye to the few passengers and crew, waving their hands nervously, or wiping tears away with white handkerchiefs, their noses reddened both by emotion and by the cold.

Our journey to the port of Esmeraldas took twenty-seven days, almost eight thousand miles, before we reached our final destination, although we made several stops in between. It was the first time we had sailed and while we were docked, I felt that the ship was like a giant house, full of containers and that no wave, no matter how big, could sink it. But on the high seas, surrounded by endless masses of water, my perception changed, and I felt like we were ants clinging to a nutshell at the mercy and whim of the waves.

Our first stop was at the port of Southampton. Upon arrival, we recalled that the legendary "Titanic" had departed from that same place on its maiden voyage, forty-two years before. But our illusion was so great that no bad omen could intimidate us. We had left behind that which most frightened us and we had no thoughts of returning under any circumstance. It was a journey of no return and we both knew it, as did our families, who deeply disagreed with our decision, albeit for different reasons.

We discussed it only the first night, with the mutual promise not to talk about it again. It bothered us both like a mosquito bite, while we watched the port recede and the yellowish gleam of its lights dim. We reached a point where we could no longer see the port and our only reference from the ship was the light of the stars in the blackness of the celestial vault. You hugged me from behind, covering me with your warm and comforting body. I felt like the luckiest person on earth and I would not trade that moment for any other in my life. I also thought that I could live the rest of my life without breaking that embrace.

Life on the ship was repetitive and one day resembled the next like two eggs from the same hen. We had breakfast at eight in the morning; we had lunch at one and dinner at seven in the evening, in the officers' mess. Always at the same table and with the same guests. Those were the rules, of which we were informed at the meeting called by the captain upon our arrival on board, before setting sail from Stockholm. There were no incidents related to the state of the sea during the crossing, since not a single storm disturbed the navigation. The days passed with sunshine and small clouds that barely moved. It was quite a contrast to the experiences we shared during the moments spent with six other diners.

In addition to the captain's table, which included the first and second officers, we shared a table with three other couples. At a certain distance there was another smaller table, known as the "cat table", due to the status of its passengers, who slept with the sailors in the berth.

After dinner we used to go on the aft deck to watch the wake of the ship, which ripped the skin of the sea in two and produced a garland of elongated white foam. There we felt free to laugh at how pretentious our table companions were. A middle-aged Danish couple, Agatha and Klaus, who came to dinner daily with all their jewelry on, as if they were walking display cases. The clinking of Agatha's bracelets as she cut the food was ostentatious and repulsive and resulted particularly annoying. Klaus wore several rings. One of them, which he wore on his left index finger, had a shield I didn't recognize which matched the one on the cover of the pocket watch that hung from his striped silk vest.

It was that Danish couple that explained to us the significance of the "cat table", as they glanced at it contemptuously, describing the well-known fact that cats licked their owners' plates when they had finished eating.

A married couple and their four sons, aged between two and eight, dined at the aforementioned table. You could clearly see their effort to keep the children seated, while the dining room employees served the main table, leaving them for last. We found out that they were Poles and we felt sorry for them. We had not forgotten the uprising in Warsaw ten years before and its destruction by the Nazis. They looked like recent refugees, sad and dignified, as they spoke in inaudible whispers. We would have preferred to share the table with them rather than with Agatha and Klaus, who embarrassed us with their arrogant behavior, but the rules on a ship are rigid and must be respected.

Our countries, Sweden and Denmark, had been enemies in the past and fought fiercely for control of the land, especially in Götaland. Although that was well behind us, many Danes still considered that it was their usurped land. History is almost always written by the victors, as is commonly known. That was never a topic of discussion between you and me.

One day at breakfast Agatha and Klaus also informed us that it was not acceptable to carry umbrellas or to whistle on ships, as both were considered bad omens. It seemed that they had dedicated their lives to collecting absurd memories.

There were two other couples. One was a medium-sized, stocky German woman. Her companion was a very skinny man, whose dry and expressionless face was transformed the moment his food was served, smiling with suppressed gluttony. When they both finished eating, they excused themselves and went back to their cabin. They were never seen on deck and the pallor of his face remained until they landed in Colón and we never saw them again.

The other couple were two very young Dutch brothers, in their twenties, with red hair and freckles on their tanned faces. They looked so happy, as if life was nothing but a fantastic adventure. Their origin from a wealthy family was evident due to the quality of their clothes; their cultured language also denoted a meticulous education. They often sat at the captain's table and talked about their father, as if he and the captain were old friends. They said that they were going to visit some relatives established in Panama, and any comment from the captain or the officers provoked a scandalous laugh that infected the rest of us. They were so young, beautiful, and unconcerned about the contingencies of life. Apparently, they had no reason to worry, although in life you never know where misfortune lurks.

The *Astrid Bakke* was not a luxury ship, but a freighter. We had seen huge bunches of bananas destined for the European population unloaded, and then manufactured products take their place on the way back to America. But we were not impressed or attracted by luxury, rather it annoyed us; we found it totally futile. In spite of it all, for us it was a beautiful trip, like a postponed honeymoon.

The New World

*T*he ship crossed the Atlantic Ocean with its cargo and we arrived at the Port of Colón when the light of day was barely shining. As they raised the Panamanian flag, with its two stars, one blue and one red, on the highest mast, we saw the shadows of the approaching city. It was slipping past us, producing a deceptive sensation that the world was moving instead of the ship. The New World welcomed us hand in hand, on the deck of the ship. The motors were stopping little by little, until they stalled completely. It was then that we perceived the intense sounds and smells of the port.

In our cabin, at least an hour before arrival, we had perceived the scent of the Caribbean. Despite the early hour, the smell was as strong as a sweet, burning slap in the face upon reaching the port. Over time we learned that it was the smell of ripe guava that was fermenting.

After that day, every time the aroma of guava reached us in all the places we traveled, we looked at each other remembering and we knew which part of our history was going through the other's head. This is how a couple's relationship is woven, by recalling shared sensations.

We toured the city throughout that day. The powerful influence of the United States could be seen everywhere. In its stores, hotels, and restaurants, whose menu cards prioritized the English language over Spanish. We tried to buy a map of the city, without success, and after lunch we returned to the ship to rest and continue our journey the following night.

It was already dawn when we marveled at the passage through Lake Gatún and the lock system, which lasted twelve hours. We finally reached the Miraflores lock, in the port of Balboa, and the Pacific Ocean opened up before our astonished eyes, flooding them with its greenish hue. It seemed to us that color was different, somewhere between green and gray. Even the previously intense smell seemed to fade. We deduced, with a happy reflection, that it was us who had assimilated tropical aromas. We were already acclimatizing, we concluded, a bit too optimistic. We had no idea what was in store for us.

We considered that Panama was too intervened by the United States and it had no attraction for us. We had already experienced the canal, whose system of locks is an amazing work of hydraulic engineering. Arriving at the Miraflores lock, after entering the port of Colón and traveling through Lake Gatún, was an experience incomparable to any previous event in our lives. At a certain distance it seemed impossible that the ship could enter that small space, as if they wanted to push through a much too narrow funnel, but to our limitless amazement everything worked with the efficiency expected by the captain.

After traversing the Panama Canal and thus crossing from the Atlantic to the Pacific Ocean, a work of magic that technology and economy were able to conjure, we headed south and on March 12 we disembarked at the seaport of Esmeraldas, in search of a Swede who owned a banana plantation.

What a great disappointment we experienced! We soon discovered that his life was not as he had painted it in the Swedish newspapers and his plantation operated under a degrading, near slavish system. Double standards were served. In Sweden he seemed like a benefactor, while in Ecuador his behavior was that of a slavedriver.

The pompous slowness of the officials, uniformed as admirals, who boarded the ship to check the passengers' documentation was grotesque. It was an exasperating situation that we would never forget. We would laugh afterwards, as we imitated their grandiloquent gestures and the movement of their dragging feet, as if they wore cement shoes. To make matters worse, we had to put up with the stench of the estuary, at twelve noon, while they reviewed each page of the passport with the slowness of an indecipherable enigma. It was a test of our resistance.

The banana plantation was not the only disappointment in Ecuador. Women continued to birth children, contradicting the laws of nature. We arrogantly consider ourselves the crown of creation, but the reality demonstrated in our day-to-day behavior belies this. Human population must not grow beyond the possibilities to offer a decent life to its descendants. Nor at the cost of land degradation, which is forced into exhaustive production to support those children who should not have been born. Women and the land have something in common: both are exploited as if their productivity were limitless. The absence of education does not allow them to analyze it, but to animals this knowledge comes naturally.

There were no fruit trees, which would be an easy food source in about ten years, because they didn't plant them. A few trees had grown spontaneously among the corn fields, which were damaged by the tools used to carelessly hill the corn plants. All the trees looked sickly. They were not good farmers. They were unaware of agrochemicals, fortunately, but they did not use compost either. They only knew the use of fresh manure, but they did not even have enough animals for an adequate supply. Misery and more misery, in any direction the eye could see.

Our pilgrimage began as we travelled through each of the Central American countries, a cultural archipelago united by language. We were shocked daily by what we witnessed and experienced. Nicaragua was gripped by an iron dictatorship under the mandate of the Somoza family. The murders and tortures were abundant in the newspapers, in the daily news and on the streets. We arrived soon after the April Revolution and the land exuded gunpowder. The dictator, who had survived an assassination attempt, kept the population at bay. They were mostly subsistence farmers, but with fallow fields that produced nothing to sustain life. In a state of war neither the fields nor life can be tended to; everything is destruction and life is buried under mountains of rubble. The absence of freedom and the repression palpable in the streets was not the harmonious and peaceful life that we were looking for.

Those dark-skinned people, small in stature but with valor beaming from their eyes, were the victims as they fell prey to their unscrupulous rulers. Not a hint of compassion was directed towards this starving, but defiant, population.

On the other hand, the fusion of priests, poets and guerrillas was difficult for us to understand. We observed everything with the best will to understand, but we would not achieve it until several years later when we met a Spanish Jesuit priest named Francisco who told us about his life in Nicaragua. I don't remember how many days we were there, but what we saw made us suffer. The impotence and frustration of the people made us want to flee because we could not ignore the suffering of any living being. We feel a great admiration for their ability to stand up to the giant that crushed them, like an ant fighting an elephant. They had our sympathies, but it was not our fight. We were looking for a place to live in peace, away from any conflict.

In El Salvador, the Legislative Assembly had passed laws abolishing communal lands which resulted in irregular distribution and sparked an uprising in an important part of the population. It broke out a few days before our arrival and fortunately we decided not to stay. Later we learned that it had been a good decision, due to the bloody civil war that ensued. I don't know why they call it "civil"; no war is.

It was not a good political moment when we set foot in Guatemala either. With the coup against the Arbenz government and the imposition of the dictatorship, once again the rifles smelled of gunpowder and the land was devastated.

The earth always pays the consequences of bad actions; it cannot flee from the violence or human greed, quite the opposite. She is a welcoming mother who always forgives abuse, time and time again. But how long can she forgive? Are there limits to her tolerance? The world is beautiful and the earth a generous matrix. But we humans pillage it down to the tiniest sediments.

We found it was not convenient to stay, although it was such a beautiful country. Color filled the clothes of its Mayan people. The women, so dignified, with their huipiles embroidered on the waist loom. They were spoken portraits, revealing their ethnic group and the hierarchy within it. It was a beautiful presentation card. But the new government had cornered the indigenous people by taking away their land, thus making them the poorest of the poor.

We were amazed at the meaning of the name Guatemala in Nahuatl: *Quauhtlemallan*, "place of many trees". We left there feeling sad, with an image implanted in our retina of a beautiful country of small, hardworking people, with a very unfair government and an unfair distribution of resources. Central America shuddered. An earthquake shot through it from north to south, from west to east. We knew that it was not a good time to arrive in this part of the world, which was in upheaval.

We spent Christmas in California that year, 1954, at the home of our friends, Ben and Ruth. Despite our friend's wishes, there was no chance we could reside there. The idea of living in a place that was already so civilized was not attractive to us, even if it was the New World. So, for the New Year we scoured the map once again. I carefully traced the unfolded map with my forefinger and slid it down the continent to Mexico. That was our next stop.

Mexico was so difficult and bureaucratic for us. Bribery was the only method to accomplish anything, and our money slipped away like water, as if we had a holes in the palms of our hands. We were desperate, but we didn't want to go back to Denmark or Sweden. We did not want to return to a life that seemed so unnatural to us.

The feature that most impressed us throughout the journey through the so-called New World was misery. When we left Sweden, we were looking for a place in the world where we could live in harmony with our future children. A place to live a healthy and respectful life, in peace. After our initial travels, we lowered our expectations and we would settle for a place where we could live, growing our own food and where our bodies could bask in the sun and fresh air for most of the year. We also decided that there were already enough creatures in the world and that the drift of the planet did not offer guarantees of a future life that matched our desires for peace and harmony with nature. Having children ceased to be a priority. We avoided them for some time, and then, for whatever reason, they never came.

That night in April 1955 a dense, uncomfortable despondency enveloped us like a heavy blanket as we laid down to sleep. We could not see a path to forward; an impregnable wall stood in front of our eyes and prevented us from imagining the horizon beyond our own nose. We were awake for more than an hour and although we didn't speak, we could tell by the sound of our breathing that we were both still ruminating on either side of the bed.

At some point during that night, I entrusted our destiny to my dreams once again since they often resolved my enigmas. I had to resort to my regular breathing to fall asleep, and it was fulfilled. It was a deep sleep that night which led me across lands and seas to an unknown territory of fertile beauty.

The next morning, I felt illuminated by the dream. It was a beautiful place between the sea and the mountains, with gigantic trees full of flowers similar to those of apple trees. I saw them in a delicate pale pink color like embroidered filigree on the tulle of a wedding dress. I knew then that it was Costa Rica because the image of a country with two peninsulas appeared in my dream. When we looked at the map, we saw it was the only country in Latin America with two peninsulas. We had no doubt what our next and hopefully final destination would be. We welcomed this thought this with a mixture of hope and concern.

That same morning, filled with enthusiasm, we went to the consulate to inquire about the required paperwork. It was all so easy, we only had to fill out a filiation document. They told us at the consulate that the country did not have an army, it had been abolished seven years earlier. It seemed to us the best path to living in peace and harmony with nature. Two months after our arrival, we saw that the flowers that had called me with their beauty were from the Rosy Trumpet Trees. We also learned months later that in January of that same year there was a failed attempt to overthrow the government of José Figueres. Sometimes it's better not to know the whole truth. Knowing this might deterred us from settling here, we avoided warlike attitudes like the plague. Despite all the difficulties and illnesses that we have suffered, we have lived the happiest years of our lives here so far. We will never know what would have happened if our decision had been different.

Costa Rica

1955

We arrived in Costa Rica on May 15, with the onset of the rainy season. Our residency cost fifty Colones each and was valid for eighteen years. When they told us at Immigration, I thought we had misunderstood the price. After travelling through Mexico everything seemed so easy and affordable.

The first place we visited was the Golfito area. I remember the incessant rain, day and night. We could imagine our fruit trees swimming towards the sea. No, that was not our place to plant fruit trees and live from them. We needed more sun. We returned to the small hotel in San José, in the Aranjuez neighborhood. The next day, they told us at the Meteorological Institute that the Nicoya Peninsula and Guanacaste were not as rainy. We headed there by bus with our illusions shaken, traversing a hellish highway which induced a headache that stayed with me for several days.

After different trials on one side of the country and the other, we finally arrived in Puntarenas one day in the month of July. The trip took several hours with many stops and in the company of chickens, baskets and milk containers. It gave us an insight to the agrarian lifestyle of the Central Valley. Puntarenas was a beautiful place, surrounded by water. A strip of land jutting out into the Pacific while the waves washed over the dark, volcanic sand on the beach.

The mangrove swamp on the other side of the strip was dotted with countless small boats of all colors, with names dedicated women *Jenny, Queen of the Sea, Angelica...* We also learned that there was a passenger train from the capital, but that day we only saw the tracks which ran parallel to the beach.

We were amazed by those wonderful trees full of orange flowers that upholstered the ground below, like the carpeted room of an Arabian sheikh. We asked a man in the seat next to us and he told us that they are called Malinche, the Royal Poinciana. I was pleased to remember that Malinche was the name of the Aztec princess, daughter of the chieftain Moctezuma. She had served as an interpreter for the Spanish conqueror Hernán Cortés and later she became his lover. When she arrived in Spain, they translated her name as Marina and those exquisite trees graced her with their beauty.

The city of Puntarenas still maintains the typical colonial structure. The church with a park in front, surrounded by houses in rows that form a square measuring one hundred meters on each side. The houses are generally small, made of wooden planks arranged horizontally and painted in bright and cheerful colors. They all have a corridor with chairs, rocking chairs and plants take up much of the space, and there are cats everywhere, laying lazily in the sun. Cats are part of the enrolled population in a fishing village.

There was a humble farmer on that bus to Puntarenas, with no shoes and worn-out clothes. He told us about the town of Montezuma and at that moment I related it to the tree and the Aztec princess. We went there, although when we arrived, we found that the farmer had deceived us when he told us that there was a hotel where we could stay. But who knows what he had understood of our questions, spoken in a Spanish as deficient as ours was back then, or what we had understood from his answers. We boarded a boat that left Puntarenas at midnight. When we got there, with no hotels in town or any other place to stay, we had no choice but to rent a house for an outrageous sum for the time: five Colones per day. A very large sum given our diminished resources.

So, we settled in Montezuma, temporarily, not knowing the span of our transience. You traveled restlessly from Montezuma to Puntarenas, searching for the right place for us to settle down permanently. One day you encountered Alejandro Pérez on the boat to Puntarenas. He boarded in Paquera and you talked the whole way. You were very happy when you returned from that trip, rubbing your hands with an audacious and triumphant air that anticipated an exciting story. We were finally starting to see the light after so much darkness.

Life was smiling at us and for a while we lived in that beautiful house on the beach in Puntarenas that the Pérez family lent us. Such generous people! While I organized the house, you traveled nonstop. Back to Montezuma and some islands in the gulf, but you couldn't make up your mind for one reason or another. We ended up on the beautiful Isla Jesusita, next to the Paquera pier. Buying it cost us seven hundred Colones, about a hundred US dollars at the time. Although today it seems like a ridiculous number, those were different times and money had a different value.

We tried to live there, but there was very little fresh water and plenty of mosquitoes. We decided to leave after two days, but it was not easy because we did not have a boat. I looked at the horizon towards Paquera, until my eyes stung from the sun and the saltpeter of the sea. Finally, when we were resigned to spend another night there, a dark-haired boy named Mario arrived in a panga to help us. The look on his face when he saw us was somewhere between curious and amused. I imagine we were outlandish in his eyes. I will remember him until the last of my days. We went to Montezuma with all our things because we recalled that there were no mosquitoes there. The mosquito plague of the last few days had seemed like punishment of biblical proportions.

In August we bought a farm, built a ranch, and channeled water to the ranch from the stream using thick bamboo shoots. We tied a canvas to some sticks, which served as our house, and immediately began planting seeds and trees. It would be a few months later, on a walk from Montezuma to El Cabo, when I saw the volcanic rock masses falling into the sea that I had dreamed of in Mexico. Yes, that was our place. I could finally show you the Paradise that I had seen in my dreams, although in my eyes

Eden was any place where you were. That was my only home, the only port where I wanted to hoist my flag.

We bought the farm from Emiliano Muñoz on August 30, 1955. With the help of several workers, we began to dig holes. Do you remember how many trees we planted? One by one, medlars, sapotes, mangoes, guavas, mamey, avocados, cashews, star apples... up to thirty-two different species. Most of the fruit trees were meant for the animals to eat.

We worked so hard building nurseries hoping that life would return to the forest from which it had fled. We had to plant enough to share with the animals of the dry forest. There was nothing left after ten years of systematic logging; just bananas.

That's what the people of Montezuma used to say. In 1945 the forest was intact, but there was nothing left to cut down when we arrived ten years later. It was all cattle pasture. Ravaging tropical forests for the benefit of a few usurpers who have nothing to do with the land, which they only loot without giving anything back. Sometimes it seems that when humanity thinks it is moving forward, it is actually moving backwards. I believe, however, that the fact that Ticos do not eat much beef is directly related to their gentle and friendly nature.

The tools sent by your father from Karl-Erik Anell's hardware store in Ulricehamn were momentous for working the land and for building our house. It took several months for the shipments to reach us, and by the time the first tools got here they were covered with rust. They looked old, as if they were bought second hand. The next shipment was vacuum packed in the hardware store and they still bore the greasy sheen of a brand-new tool when we opened them.

Between 1967 and 1971 we began purchasing land from our neighbors. Thus, piece by piece, we linked more than sixty-two hectares, dedicated exclusively to wildlife. I remember everything clearly.

That was the purpose of my father's inheritance, to bring a piece of the forest back to life. My father regretted that I abandoned my family so intensely, as my brothers and his damned widow never ceased to remind me. That's what you call my stepmother, the damned widow, never by her name. It was your way of complaining when she tried to withhold my share of the inheritance.

We managed to unite several farms and create a larger one, with three natural limits: a stream to the north, another to the west and on the southern limit the sea. The east, which was in the forest, was the only boundary shared with other landowners.

In this simple way, without doing anything directly, we allowed sovereign nature to replenish the wildlife, which returned little by little, at a slow but continuous pace. It is surprising how animals know that their habitat is expanding and with the expansion of their habitat their lives improve. They reproduce when conditions improve, it is only then that they have litters again, never in situations of scarcity or danger. It is something so easy for them to understand, but it is astounding that this very basic canon of survival is not understood by humans. I imagine that the intervention of the Church and its precepts and interference in the lives of the parishioners has something to do with it.

Agriculture and livestock were progressive for human settlers, but regressive for the rest of the living species. By removing the forest and destroying its habitat, the animals no longer had a place to hide from human predation.

Here, in Cabo Blanco, when they chose a tree to cut down, they cut all the surrounding trees, so that it could fall. Everything had to be cut. The saws rattled with their irritating screech for days on end. From time to time the warning shouts were heard, "Tree goes!", then the ferocious crash. For a time, only silent death spoke. Then on to the next tree, until all the ancient trees that inhabited the forest were annihilated.

We were told that the huge trunks of mahogany, ron-rón and nazareno were dragged slowly by several pairs of oxen to the pier, sometimes for five or seven days. The load was so heavy that the axles of the wheels broke sometimes, and the transport had to be stopped until it was repaired. Time had a different dimension and if the task required it, no one questioned the hours or days spent on the transport operation.

At the pier, ropes soaked in salt water held the trunks with one end while the other end was tied to the boat. The boat waited in the ocean, away from the surf of the shore, while a man rode on the trunk to hold the rope so it wouldn't slip. He had to be very brave and a good swimmer, because the surging waves continually threw him into the water. One of them was called Fausto and he came from Limón. He was a short black man, very brave and permanently angry, with the temperament of the devil. Another had the last name Vargas, but I forgot his first name. His work was not finished until the trunk was brought alongside the boat. "You see, those surfers who have been arriving recently haven't invented anything new", the old men of the place repeated sarcastically to anyone who would listen. We all laughed at their tales, but the forest was exterminated. The loggers and their laborers left and the town was deserted.

Karen with a breadfruit

Cabo Blanco

*V*íctor Bravo was the first person to settle here. He was Nicaraguan and arrived in 1916 on a sailboat that he built himself, according to his account. He lived with his family on the land that is now our farm. His eyes shined with emotion when he described to us all the animals that could be found when it was a virgin forest here: jaguars, macaws, and toucans in huge flocks. He said that at night you could hear the howls of the jaguars, like the songs of life. We listened to his stories, enraptured, while he spoke with that Nicaraguan accent which is so different from the Tico accent. His features, with high cheekbones and tanned skin, were quite the opposite to the descendants from the Spaniards. Honorable hallmarks of his heritage.

At that time, the land was quite fertile and many varieties of grains were grown. Sacks and sacks of rice, corn and beans were sent to Puntarenas every week by boat. We were one of the grain producers of the country. Montezuma seemed like a small city to us, with grocery stores, a pharmacy, a post office and even a shoe store. It really was the central core of the area's economic nucleus. Precious carts came from Río Negro de Arío, Playa Naranjo, Paquera, Cóbano and other places, each trying to outdo the other with the decoration of their wooden wheels, artistically painted with elliptical figures and a profusion of tropical colors, reminiscent of beautiful mandalas. The carts were pulled by pairs of oxen, which transported huge quantities of sacks of rice, beans, and corn to other towns. In exchange, they brought pigs, chickens, and cows to sell here.

There were two market days; Monday and Thursday, and the moans of the carts blended with the neighs of the horses and the cries of the people selling rice, corn, beans, chickens, and pigs. All that food was produced, in huge quantities, to feed the attendees. Freshly palmed tortillas and mincemeats of different tubers. In short, things that we would never have even imagined.

Despite all that activity two days a week, the rest of the time we were very isolated from the rest of the country and the continent, as if what happened in the outside world was irrelevant. As if we lived on another planet.

I recall the day you went to Cabo Blanco to look for red sapote seeds, one day in early December 1960. Your eyes were radiant and you were so excited when you came back! You had discovered an area of the forest that was still intact. Seeing a large herd of coatis pass by made you think: if the forest disappeared, where would the animals live? You were determined when came home. You had to do something to save the remaining forest. We had no peace from that day on because we pondered constantly what we could do to save that beautiful forest.

It all started with the first letter. It was at midnight on December 26, 1960 when you began to put out a distress call, at the suggestion of our friends Ben and Ruth from California.

I evoke in my memories the passion with which you wrote ten years before, by the light of an oil lamp. You told me, with a hint of irony shining in your smiling eyes and in the corner of your lips, that you had to touch the hearts of old and rich European widows. You had such a mischievous expression...they would understand our love for animals, just as they loved their fluffy angora cats, snuggled up in their warm laps. I laughed so hard that I was still laughing as I fell asleep in bed.

The first donation was ten pounds, which came by way of Stella Lief. We immediately named her honorary secretary. Over time, we would name one of the hills in the reserve in her honor. She asked you to send her a detailed history of Cabo Blanco, so that she could use it to generate interest in the reserve. I still remember the letter today, with emotion beaming in every one of my particles.

It is written with that revealing passion of yours. No one who read it could resist your deep emotion. I can see you while you searched within yourself for the most intimate words that could touch hearts and move them.

...we feel a duty to help abused horses and dogs, as well as to freed captive animals. We can free small birds instantly; however, parrots need to be cared for until their flight feathers have grown back (they are almost always clipped). Every time we go to work or to inspect the property, we bring the parrots and put them in a nearby tree, where they eat flowers, seeds, and berries. They look so excited and happy! When wild birds take flight, our pupils also

try to fly, but fall to the ground because their flight feathers have been removed...

All your gestures towards animals are impregnated with a delicacy and sensitivity born of your deep love for them, and they reciprocated that love tenfold.

Then followed, a series of very emotional letters to conservation organizations in England and the United States in which you requested help to save what was left of the forest in Cabo Blanco. The response was quick and positive: they would send us the money once there was a commitment from the Government of Costa Rica to preserve the land.

It was a surprise when all the associations responded with an interest in sending money, but the Government clashed with them, warning that although it did accept the proposal, nothing would be done until the money was here.

It was then that your pilgrimage to San José began, to the newly founded Institute of Lands and Colonization. They would have to draw up a plan of the area that would be expropriated, and a document detailing the commitment between the State and the conservation associations *Philadelphia Conservationists, Seattle Lovers and Friends of Nature*, and *Nature Conservancy*. Getting all the parties to agree meant three years of negotiations, in which you acted as a messenger, at times disheartened and with broken wings. The Government of Costa Rica would not accept the requirements of the associations before the money was in its coffers and the associations would not send the money until they had a commitment from the government. This is how the three years passed, in this game of Ping-Pong.

They were three years of madness and desperation, with continuous trips to San José. You made at least thirteen trips that I can recall. Meanwhile, the forest was disappearing, day by day, due to felling for the sale of wood. It was a no man's land when it came to protection, but a free for all when it came to exploitation to the point of absolute annihilation. There were some moments when the terrible feeling of hopelessness overcame us. We feared that there would be nothing left to protect. They cut trees relentlessly during those three years. Ironically, at the time it was common for people to demolish a virgin forests and claim that this represented "improvements" to a property, for which they obtained benefits from the State due to the so-called Possessory Information Law. What a criminal inconsistency.

Little by little, we got to know the fifteen families who were settled in what is now the reserve. They lived in houses they had built themselves with wooden poles which were harvested by felling the trees. The walls and ceilings were made of straw or palm leaves with earthen floors. It was a single space where they cooked, slept, and procreated. Sometimes, while the houses were being built, the whole family, including babies and old people, slept under a tree. They stepped onto the dirt floor of their house once the wooden walls and palm roofs were ready. One of these families were the Castros, who came from San Ramón. When we met them, they were living under a tree, luckily it was dry season. When the rains came, they were already living in their little ranch.

Also, from that moment on, young coatis, raccoons and parrots were left at our house by the neighbors, day after day, like a continuous drip. They found them in the forest and after a while it became problematic to have them in the house, because they could not live as pets.

It was a problem brought on by human's predatory model of life, who will not accept the consequences of their actions. We realized that if they continued destroying the forest, these animals would have no place to live. Buying the land was urgent, so we could allow life to multiply at its own rhythm, without human intervention. The problem was that we did not have the money to purchase it on our own.

It was a monumental effort, but we accomplished our goal. If memory serves me, it was on February 13, 1963, when Decree number 10 created the first nature reserve in Costa Rica: The Cabo Blanco Absolute Natural Reserve, giving rise to what would later become the System of Reserves and National Parks. From then on we developed a good friendship with Allston Jenkins, the president of the Philadelphia Conservationists. Our friendship was consolidated when he came to sign the partnership agreement with the Ministry of Agriculture and Livestock. They sent a bunch of officials from the ministry who didn't even get off the boat, which was docked in front of Balsitas beach. You and I looked at each other bewildered; we couldn't understand why they had come all this way if they had no interest in seeing the land that was to be protected. We wondered what the articles contained in the agreement with the conservationist associations with which they were going to sign a contract meant to them.

I remember a photograph in which you are sitting next to María Buchinger, the Argentine activist who defends National Parks, and Álvaro Rojas, head of planning for the Costa Rican Ministry of Agriculture and Livestock. You and María are laughing while Álvaro is looking at the camera very serious, as if your laughter was completely unrelated to him.

We reached the Minister of Agriculture, Adriano Urbina through Andrés Challe. I can almost picture him on the dock in Puntarenas, standing on the deck of his yacht *Papagayo* and wearing his captain's cap, barking orders left and right.

We accomplished it working together, although it was not an easy feat. It required hundreds of hours and days of conversations, in which we suffered because we could not understand the lentitude of the process. Despairing at the disaster that was allowed to continue while they dithered. It was in plain sight, but hardly anyone wanted to see it, and the predators took advantage of it, slashing as fast as their tools and greed would allow. The Laws themselves favored the felling of trees as an "improvement" of the farms. As such, they put all their efforts into the unlimited felling of the trees, which were falling without respite, in the hope that these "improvements" would be calculated into the value of the land at the time of the expropriation. In the end, we only managed to save 15% of the primary forest of Cabo Blanco.

It would be a long time before the law that protects natural resources, considered today an essential element of all Costa Rican citizens, was put into practice. Which shows that customs lead to laws, but it is more difficult to cultivate customs than it is to make laws.

Sadly, after all these years, this is still the case. Only a few of us truly feel that the earth is our nurturing Mother.

When the money finally arrived, the expropriation of the squatters was managed by the Government. Some of them were paid with State Bonds for a value of 75% of the appraisal. Although they were squatters and did not have property titles, some of the expropriated people got angry and clashed with us. They called us thieves and blamed us for what they considered a low price for their expropriation. They literally said "Nicolás scammed us". We were the true victims of the Government's trap, caught in the crossfire, taking shots from both sides.

I was surely spared due to their own machismo, because I was a supposedly harmless woman. They did not know the different ways I could fight, nor did they know my determination to fulfill our desire. They could not intuit that we had burned our vessels when leaving Sweden and that prevented us from even looking back. Not even fear, which we felt, especially at night, could stop us from continuing. The unappealable decision to fight for what we considered fair and our compassion for the inhabitants of the forest gave us the courage that we possibly lacked. For some time, we lived on permanent alert, always attentive to strange noises. It was exhausting. We moved to the house on the hill and built a palisade around it, like a western-style fort. The threats were serious and launched from different fronts, depending on the interests that drove them.

After the expropriation, we agreed on a protection system with the Government using park rangers. It had to be an absolute reserve, without tourist visits, but that was a non-existent concept in the country. It was then that the disagreement between the English and North American conservation associations arose, which lasted more than seven years. During this time, on more than one occasion we believed that the project would flounder, although we had no intention of giving up on it.

I remember the nervous emotion when the decree was finally issued that registered Cabo Blanco as the first absolute reserve on October 21, 1963. It had been pouring rain all month and we had hardly any dry clothes to change into, but it was one of the happiest days of our lives.

Nicolás working in the corn field

I find you

I snapped back to reality when I heard one of the young boys call the man by his name: "Don Emiliano, come here" and they walked off, side by side. The boy spoke while the other listened attentively. They returned to get me quickly, with grave looks on their faces and their hats in their hands. At that moment I knew that something bad, perhaps terrible, had happened. The worst premonitions flashed through my memory like the scenes of a movie.

There are times when you know things are going wrong; your instinct tells you, you feel it in your skin, even in the air you breathe. You know that you have arrived too late and you wish the scenario in which you are featuring was in the past. Run. Run from the scene so this event does not affect you and does not become part of your history. Perturbed, you wish to desert your own novel, forgo the role of protagonist.

How many of us wish to protect everything we love with all our might, even though we know it is impossible because we lack that power. We understand our condition as mortals, but still, we strive for the immortality of those we love. In that sense, we are so different than other animals.

In nature there is no right or wrong. It is only one lifeform fighting another lifeform, striving for survival, for continuance. Life consumes life, an intermittency repeated in perpetuity. The endless musical score of Life/Death/Life; an infinite waltz. The cycles are completed, without courting or considering our intervention.

My ponderings were interrupted by the older man's voice, which sounded as if it emerged from a cave, when he said: "We found your husband, but he is dead and…" Before he could finish, I ran in the direction where they had been and less than two-hundred meters away I found the remains of your clothes and your scattered bones. The anticipated calamity was fiercely transforming into reality. I cursed at the vultures, still strutting around your remains, and I plunged into the most tenebrous horror.

Never in my worst nightmares did I foresee the dimension of the tragedy unfolding before me. I could have never sensed the utter devastation to which you fell victim. I felt the spiral of delirium engulfing me. A nightmare made flesh so I could contemplate it in its most macabre manifestation.

My voice broke and I could not even scream, although tears drowned my eyes and erased my face. The remains of your skull left me no doubts. In that moment I felt the black abyss of death growing inside me, eating a hole in me, suctioning my vital essence, leaving me without consistency.

I was still unwilling to accept the reality of the scene, but your shredded clothes, your hat, and your identification card confirmed that the bare bones laying on the ground were yours. Your skull had a hole from an incision and the older man, unflappable, said it looked like a wound caused by a falling branch: "An untimely death" he concluded. The word "untimely" echoed in my head and began winding down from my brain to my entrails and tore me up perversely. I could feel the absence of your life inside my body and I was contaminated by your death.

Nobody is prepared for death, and I certainly was not. I bowed, shattered by the blow of your death rattle. Is it possible to die by intensely wishing for death? Nietzsche said: "And if thou gaze long into the abyss, the abyss will also gaze into you." I wanted to gaze at death face to face so that death could gaze at me, but death was not there. She was gone, clasping her prey in her jaws: you. You were the prey, and I, unsuspecting, was left ravaged.

I lost track of what the boys and the middle-aged man were telling me. Something about filing a report, but for what? Who but me should receive a report of your death? Who but me is concerned about your death?

I made a titanic effort to think logically and follow the law. The Criminal Investigation Unit would send detectives to investigate the cause of your death, although it seemed that it was caused by a falling branch. The middle-aged man solemnly referred to a similar case in Sirena, as he looked into my eyes, which were blinded by tears.

I realized, in a moment of sanity, that my life would never be the same again, not even in Paradise. The grief from your death became my undiagnosed disease. My sickened entrails writhed in pain as I knelt on the blood red earth and picked up your identification card and your hat. I pressed them against my chest and buried my face in them, searching for the remains of your scent.

I knew this was "evidence", but I refused to leave them. Evidence of what? Of your presence there? It was all I could conserve of you, the tracks of your final moments of life. They no longer housed the sublime levity of your untamed soul.

Time, which I thought to be my ally during the trip, had not been on my side. Not on this occasion. I cursed Cronos for having tricked me with the illusion that the dimension of time would remain still until I found you. I could not leave your remains, although the protocols of the investigation would require it. Your remains had nourished wild animals. It was small consolation in the face of this tragic horror. You had not chosen your death, but I knew this was how you would have wanted to perish: nourishing the wildlife. You had told me once, when we settled in Cocalito, to bury only your clean bones, the flesh should feed the animals. I never knew how I could manage to fulfill your wish, but life, in its wisdom, had accomplished the task.

The boys had returned to the ranches to find a sack for your bones as I sat on the ground where the remains of your blood were visible. I ran my fingers over the dried blood again and again, loosing track of time. Nothing mattered now.

When they returned, I could not tell if they were gone for an hour or an instant. The passing of time no longer mattered to me. The future did not exist, and the past did not need time, only memory. New events occur and they nullify old events. So, what would need to happen to nullify what was annihilating me now?

They brought back a sack that had held cement. "It was the only thing we could find", the boys said awkwardly. I shook out the dust that was still inside while my heart and my mind engaged in a frantic struggle between logic and dismay. A vortex of confused thoughts scattered out in every direction; dispersing in flocks with no determined path to follow. It demanded a diligence of which I was incapable, augmented by the unbearable and dismal undertaking of having to store your remains in such an undignified vessel.

My pain increased into a wound of incomprehensible magnitude and infinite extension. I had transformed into ambulant wound, with nothing salvageable of my anatomy. It was useless attempting to apply logic to your death. I could not accept that we would never be "us" again.

On the way back to the ranches I considered suicide as an alternative to this brutal pain; death would be a solid comfort. On this occasion, however, I could not make self-serving decisions. Suicide is not an alternative. I can recognize through my haze that there is something more pressing. Why did I allow you to come here alone? Why?

I think perhaps this would not have happened if I had been with you. We could have defended ourselves together or died together, together forever. Perhaps life had decided, without considering our opinion, that one of us had to remain. I cannot understand why I was chosen, knowing that you are stronger and more capable.

The thought of living without you terrifies me. Dying is nothing compared to not seeing you, not touching you, not smelling you….! All the words I hear inside and outside of my head are superfluous in the face of my catastrophe. I look to other words for relief from this tsunami that drowns me inwardly. Words from the spirit of *Hamlet* came to me, compounding my madness:

If I weren't forbidden to tell you the secrets of purgatory, I could tell you stories that would slice through your soul, freeze your blood, make your eyes jump out of their sockets, and your hair stand on end like porcupine…

That is exactly how I felt. The hair on my skin standing on end, like a victim as it senses the ferocity of its predator. I could not discern how much of the horror I was observing and how much I imagined. I became an unwitting hostage of the spiral tormenting my ceaseless thoughts. I could not stop the tortuous, agony of thought. I begged, uncertain to whom or what, for an instant of calm at the pinochle of the ascent of my musings. A momentary truce where everything ceases, including the beating of my heart, and lets me breathe, if reluctant death will not heed my call…

When we returned with the sack to the ranches, the proprietor looked at me with strange hostility, although perhaps it was his reaction to my crazed look and exhausted pain. Perhaps it was my warped perception of reality, which made me see enemies everywhere. I understood and determined, in each of my cells, that the most sublime bits of heaven and the most frightful bits of hell are inside every one of us. The most repulsive underworld had invaded my scene.

I decided to sleep in the ranch where the two boys lived that night, thinking the presence of children would protect me against a possible aggression. When the guide explained to the owner of the ranch about our find he did not seem surprised. He did not even look at me when I asked him if we could send someone with a message to the police post in Puerto Jiménez. I would remain there with your bones until they returned.

My nightmares blended with reality that night. My legs could no longer support my body, so I hugged my travel bag and laid back. My mind was like a sponge, soaked with insane ideas which jumped constantly from one lobe to another. I don't know if I dreamt during the time I slept, in the grips of exhaustion. I rose while it was still dark, to the howls of the Mantled Howlers, and headed to the beach. The ocean would help bring me serenity.

The next morning, the guide who helped find you said your murderer was Omar, the stepson of Enrique, the owner of the ranches. I was horrified to realize that I had slept in your murderer's own home. He was nineteen years old and he lived in Pavas. Enrique's new wife said that you had gone to the forest together, and Omar had returned on his own.

That same night, after a few drinks, his father confessed to his drinking companions. I don't know if I will ever know the truth of what happened that day, or what is hidden behind the truth. I could not believe, however, that someone who had never seen you before would want to kill you, unless he was a hired to do it. And if he was a hired killer, who hired him and why? Who pronounced the words "kill him" without feeling their weight on his conscience?

Now it's all over. I am compelled to chronicle our tragedy. There are roles that no one would ever want to have to interpret, as in this case. Although I know I can't change the course of events, I would sign a pact with anyone, in heaven or in hell, if I could return to the precise moment when we arrived at Playa Llorona. I wish I could stop time forever, in the interval in which we sighted the beach and the ranch. Because at that time I was ignorant of the horror that I am living.

The killer is captured

I waited in vain for the police to arrive from Puerto Jiménez. When the first boat arrived, I decided to travel to Cuidad Cortés to file a report with the bones in a cement sack. They would tell me what to do there, what procedure had to be followed, the "standard operating procedure", as the man in the ranch called it.

They took my statement when I arrived at the police station and I was informed that the Criminal Investigation Unit would send detectives to investigate. It was not determined when they would visit the crime scene, as was mandated by the Judicial Authority of Cuidad Cortés. They were very busy and the institution did not have the vehicles required for the detectives to make the journey. They would let me know when a date for the visit had been set.

After an unending number of days, whose count I had forgotten, I needed to shower and change my clothes. I returned to Puntarenas to the home of the Díaz family, who sheltered me with the indispensable compassion and affection the situation merited. I had to leave your bones in Ciudad Cortés, under police custody, until investigators arrived from San José.

A few days later, the three detectives landed in Río Claro and from there they flew to Punta Llorona in a small aircraft owned by a North American. It took them more than one week to reach the scene of the crime. During that week, the days that passed seemed longer than 24 hours, unending. Nobody had any sense of urgency. It was only I who could not regain my reason or find any peace waiting for the call to return to the scene of the crime.

Salvador Díaz joined me on the reconnaissance trip to the forests of Corcovado with the detectives. The investigators spent four days inspecting the area and collecting evidence. I told them I had your hat and identification card, but I would only hand them over if they promised to return them. They reminded me drily that I should not have touched them, but they could not sustain my deranged, furious gaze and agreed to the deal.

We had to reconstruct the scene of the crime. We laid the bones back on the ground, where they were, as best as the guides and I could recall. They took photographs of the scattered bones as well as the burlap sack where we collected them afterwards. We all departed to Puntarenas, and then on to San José. It took five days to get the results from the autopsy. The conclusions of the forensic doctors in San José pointed to Omar, the young man who served as your guide, as the presumptive murderer. He was the stepson of the owner of the ranches and the prime suspect of having caused your death on July 23rd at 10:00 AM; the day after you arrived. And so, it was officially certified.

When I heard the date, I recalled it was that night when the strange dreams about you began. I understood that our connection had been broken. How could I have felt you if you were no longer here?

The presumed murderer was captured by the same investigators in a house in Villa Esperanza, Pavas, where he lived with a very young girl. She was almost a child, with astonished, fearful, charcoal eyes and a thin, brown face. He offered no resistance when they arrested him.

The investigators allowed me to accompany them during the arrest. I wanted to ask him why he murdered you. I also wanted the details of your death. Had it been an agonizing death, or was it treacherously quick, with only but a moment of devastating pain? I wished that it had been the later and that your final moments of life had passed without suffering the torments of your conscience.

I heard him clearly when he said: "It took you a long time to get here, I was expecting you days ago." He calmly admitted having committed the crime, as if confessing brought him a sense of relief. He confessed that he split your head open with a machete as you watched a troop of monkeys, then clubbed your head to finish the job.

When you fell, he stabbed you in the heart with your own army issue knife, which I later found sticking out of the wild cashew tree. How to comprehend such merciless, excessive barbarism? He said he did not know why he killed you, "It was an instantaneous impulse." It was all he said, even though they asked him again and again, at his house and later at the station. So, I was left with this doubt that torments my existence: did you have a quick death or was it a slow agony? He simply would not say anything else.

I could not accept this simple explanation. I suspected that this murder could have been "by request" and he was just the executioner, but the police did not want to consider my opinion. I insisted they speak with the girl he lived with and the people who employed him or that they investigate if he had foreign friends with interests in the lumber industry. Even the gold panners and the hunters had a motive to wish for your demise. The gold panners thought that the hills of Corcovado were filled with gold, which would be dragged into their greedy hands by the strong currents of the rivers as they rushed to the sea. There were so many potential enemies, it was impossible to include them all in a single list…

At some point during my tribulations, I thought about those that the government had expropriated to form the Cabo Blanco Reserve. Some of those squatters had relocated to Corcovado to continue their practice of felling trees and selling the wood. Your presence was a threat to their lumber business, once again you attacked their means of subsistence head on. Perhaps this time they had decided not to forgive you. Now you see, my thoughts are like dark birds, restlessly beating their wings, coming and going without repose, without answers.

I wish that some compassionate person, who had lived through a similar experience, would tell me candidly how they made it through their episode and what they leaned on for support in order to survive. It would help calm my anxiety to know that one day even the most terrifying events can be confined to the past.

I distressingly recalled a few violent altercations with our neighbors when their cattle invaded our farm, which left them terribly upset. At the time, the mutual threat of gunfire made me shake with anger and with fear that such a threat would be fulfilled. You had earned some dangerous enemies with the belligerence which characterized you while defending wildlife and you never accounted for the consequences that it could bring.

No. I could never accept that that young man was your murderer. He may have committed the act, as he confessed, but nobody kills another person without a reason; without obtaining a reward that compensates for the guilt of committing such a malevolent act. I wish I knew who profited from your death so I could have them investigated. The list of those who benefited from your death would not be easy to compile if there was a will to do it. I will not let myself be convinced nor resign myself to accept the simple conclusions that place the blame solely on Omar. They were too quick to accept him as a scapegoat. What did they offer him in exchange for your life? Who had arranged this act while cloaked in the shadows?

Your funeral

I cannot cease to imagine the moment of the attack, your defensive reaction, if there even was one. From the moment of the aggression until you stopped defending yourself and lost consciousness, feeling nothing: no fear, no pain. I think in desperation what might have gone through your mind in the last moments, when you knew it was the end. Were your final moments reserved for me?

Later I was informed that police posts all over the country received reports of daily killings. "All you have to do is read the newspapers. They are filled with photos of people killed in unusual, inexplicable circumstances", the policeman said as he took my statement, attempting to console me. For them it was just another death, another form to fill out. I could not accept their indifference, however, because neither the dead nor the pain were their own. Their job was to report it, nothing else. They had no sentimental or familial relation with the dead, but I did. I had lost half of me, and I would not relent until I found the guilty party. It turned my stomach. I felt nausea building and I asked to speak to the chief of police. The officer stood up, looking annoyed, and headed towards a door at the end of the room, dragging his feet as he walked. He spoke to someone behind the closed door in a low voice. He returned after his conversation and led me to an office occupied with a dirty table strewn with papers.

The chief of police gestured for me to sit in an empty chair. He was a fat man in a military uniform which looked like it might burst at the seams at any moment. He reiterated that the motive was money, that the criminal, Omar, thought you had money. He even lowered his tone, as if revealing a secret:

"I apologize for the impropriety, ma'am, but he had a lover and she asked him for money. I was on the brink of murder myself, on two occasions, because I needed money for a woman. I nearly lost my mind."

Despite his discretion, I begged him to continue the investigation. I told him I would pay, but he would not listen. It was obvious that he wanted to forget the case, for some unknown reason, and he could not conceal it. He could not hide that knew more than he let on. He could not look me in the eyes and I decided that as long as I had strength I would not give up until I found your killers.

Despite my fatigue, I managed to gather enough strength to make a statement to the press waiting for me outside the police station.

"As long as I have strength in my body, I will continue to search for my husband's true murderers in hope that they will be punished for this inexplicable crime. I will continue Nicolas' work, alone or with the youth of this country, which is about to succumb if we do nothing to protect it. I place my trust in the younger generations, because we can expect neither respect nor justice from the older ones."

Afterwards, as I waited for them to turn over your remains, I was moved to see a story on the cover of the newspaper which confirmed my perception about the young and old generations: *There is a revolt throughout Central America and the borders are on alert. A student protest on July 30th denouncing human rights violations in the capital of El Salvador culminated in a terrible massacre. The students were surrounded by tanks, attacked with tear gas, and murdered in cold blood by the National Guard and the National Police. The number of dead is still unknown.*

I was horrified, but I could not accumulate any more suffering. I folded the newspaper so I didn't have to look at it. I was suffering from an overdose of violence. Fatigue had broken my will. I wanted to close my eyes so as not to see the evil, hear the evil, or speak of it, like the three mystic monkeys. Could that be possible?

They certified your remains on August 13th and returned your bones in the burlap sack two days later, so I could bury you in our farm. You had shown me the spot once, when we spoke about the possibility of one of us dying before the other. A special permit from the Costa Rican president was required, which I obtained through our relationship with the parents of the former first lady. Despite my insistence on finding the people responsible for your death, those who remained hidden in the shadows, I could not get them to appoint an investigator to continue with the inquiries. A confession from a guilty party had invalidated any further action, it was the perfect excuse to bury all additional enquiries. Someone had planned it that way and everyone else had conjured up this fabricated truth.

I felt like the most unfortunate woman on the planet when I climbed up the hill on August 22nd, carrying the burlap sack. I was talking to myself, giving myself orders the whole time, because I needed to hear a voice to guide me. Even if it was my own voice, like an automaton. I know not where I found the strength to dig such a deep hole, with that huge pickaxe, almost as tall as I was. I embraced you tenderly, remembering you as you were, well aware that this would be the last embrace of what was left of you before depositing your bones, with the loving care and compassion that I felt for you, and you had felt for me.

I poured earth on them and planted a small tree, the one with the white flowers, your favorite since we arrived here. Not another track would mark your grave. I realized that our lives are filled with symbols, gestures directed towards others. This was the last symbol I could dedicate to you. It would grow next to you until I could lay by your side. I had left you with the best companion. I was certain that every creature in the forest knew you were there, with them forever.

The trial and sentencing

Olof, an old saying states that time will take its course, and so, the day of the trial arrived on Thursday November 20th. The trial was fast and expedient. The murderer had confessed and had been held in prison for three months prior to the trial. He did not modify his initial statement in his confession, alleging the same motive for committing the crime: "I killed him for no other reason other than because I felt like it."

His stupid reasons convince no one. They cannot even be considered reasons. They could be considered causes, but without merit; without any logic of reasoning that could have indicated a motive for the murder. It was his truth, but it was an unbelievable truth. The truth of a madman or an idiot. He will go to prison, but he would have been better served in an insane asylum.

The sentence was read quickly. With the author of the crime established, there was nothing left to discuss or to ponder. Perhaps it was better this way, to put an end to this hopeless misfortune. There was a strange feeling of emptiness after the sentence. This moment is of maximum importance to the victims; it is that moment which marks a before and after in their expectations of the crime which was perpetrated.

All the suppositions that justice will fulfill what is expected of her are suspended in that moment of silence, awaiting the sentence that will punish the author of the crime. It is the vertex between before and after, the point of no return, the impossibility to unsay what was said, just as a fired bullet cannot reenter the chamber. From that moment forward, presumptions cease to be, changing instead to guilty or innocent. A single word changes life forever from that moment forward.

For the judges, however, the significance does not go beyond their daily duty, an action already included in their salary. Indeed, the glorified role of the judge in the process does not amount to much more than that. This is not Mount Olympus, where the gods could recur to ploys or subterfuges to palliate or bless the unappealable sentence of Zeus, their god and judge.

In the previous days, the newspapers had speculated as to the number of years of the sentence. They spoke of twenty-five years, which seemed too few to me, because he would have the opportunity to live freely afterwards, while you would not. The lawyer and I waited impatiently for the confirmation. While it would not bring you back to life, I needed for justice to be served. I needed it to show me that brutality cannot violate the right to life and to restore my confidence in the human conscience and the judicial system.

The judge looked up and with a raspy voice ordered the accused to stand. He shot up like a spring, in unison with his lawyer: "Omar López Arias, you have been found guilty and are condemned to..." Eight years! I could not bring myself to believe it. I wanted to think I had misunderstood the ruling. Was such clemency possible? A mere eight years in prison in exchange for your life, Olof. Can somebody tell me if there is any justice in this world? There is no one to answer, but I say no. There is none, and I don't want to live in a country where your murder can go unpunished. I cannot go on living my life side by side with the accomplices. I feel cornered, with no alternatives to leave but terrified to stay.

In the following days, the newspapers offered all kinds of controversial commentaries and opinions implying that the mastermind who paid to have you killed was being shielded. They were convinced, as was I, that Omar was only the executioner, the perpetrator, given that he had no reason to take your life. It is well known, however, that there are others with plenty of reasons. Some speculated that once he was incarcerated in the Penitentiary, confronting captivity in his prison hell, he would redress and reveal the truth. Perhaps he would finally reveal who prompted him to commit such a vile and despicable crime. Yes, maybe he would come clean, if those responsible don't kill him first. Impunity has existed as long as the planet has.

I listened to the journalists, illuminated by the flashes from the cameras, speak over each other in the halls of the court. The lawyer walked next to me slowly as they approached us, as if she was eager to answer their questions. They all spoke simultaneously, but all I wanted was to disappear, to flee without saying a word to anyone. It was not the time for making statements, I was dumbfounded by the leniency of the sentence. I walked quickly, with long strides, towards the door; I could hear the lawyer's high heels clicking behind me.

I was exhausted due to the insomnia of the previous nights. Once in the taxi, I threw the lawyer a stunned gaze. She looked into my eyes, smiling triumphantly, and assured me that this was a victory and that the sentence was fair and legal. I don't know what legality she referred to, or in which court this resolution is defensible. I could not have disagreed with her more and my ire was boiling over. I was unable to express myself precisely in a language I did not dominate as well as I would have liked on this occasion. It is true that anger helps us push through difficult moments, but I could not contain myself. I felt like I might levitate in an ocean of injustice, although later I would crumble.

I recalled what Karen Blixen, my compatriot, used to say about the difference between the laws of domestic animals and wild animals: "domestic animals are bound by the laws of respectability and wild animals are bound by the laws of decency." It seemed like the laws of humanity followed this rule: some humans were respectable, others just pretended. Decency is a higher state which has no place in euphemisms or masquerades.

Nobody has the right to infringe upon the integrity, or end the existence of another, without facing the consequences for taking a life inopportunely.

"Many die too late, others die too soon. Die at the right time", Zarazushtra said to Nietzsche. But is it possible, as the argument suggests, to learn how to die? What scale is used by judges to measure the magnitude of guilt for the loss of life, that which is most valuable to all living beings, at the hands of another? Are judges, mere mortals made of flesh and bone, imperfect and flawed like all others, capable of this compensatory arithmetic that determines the length of the sentence of incarceration compared to the loss of a life cut short?

I would not wish to reestablish the retributive justice of the biblical law of talion "an eye for an eye, a tooth for a tooth" because in the end we would all be blind, fumbling in a world of darkness in search of mash to eat. But he who has committed the crime will one day regain his life; he who has died will be dead forever. Those who loved him or were loved by him will never regain this love, that continuous energy that binds us in an infinite circuit.

In this case the accused, Omar, was not perturbed when he heard the guilty verdict and the sentence imposed, as if going to prison was a field trip. He was either crazy or unconscious. Perhaps he was expecting a longer sentence and was relieved to hear the lightness of his punishment...perhaps he awaited a promised indulgence, when things settled down and his co-conspirators, hiding in the shadows, had to opportunity to get him out of prison. Perhaps he trusted in a reprieve, custom-made in the shadows, because I had no doubt there was a pact to cover up your death.

But what bothered me the most was our lawyer's satisfaction with the sentence, and I made sure she knew it. She looked at me as if

I was an extraterrestrial that spoke in an incomprehensible jargon. I lack the docile, conformist personality expected of a woman. They thought it was a strange anomaly that I should keep my composure instead of being reduced to tears. I don't want to show them my grief, even though internally I am crushed. I have heard them refer to it as the "coldness" of foreigners. They don't understand that the suffering is the same, it lodges in the same place. The difference is how you choose to manifest it to the world, which face of the prism reflects our suffering. I do not seek compassion, I seek justice.

I need to regain my strength so I can formulate a strategy to search for your killers and to find another lawyer to appeal this ridiculous sentence. I must think with a clear head, but where should I start?

For a long time, I obsessed with the idea of appealing the sentence, but after meditating on it day and night for months I decided to desist because nothing and no one would bring you back to life. I was obliged, morally and physically, to continue living, there was no turning back. When we arrived from Europe we thought we would never return. Years later we eliminated any possibility of returning: we burned our vessels.

On March 25th, 1971, your father sent us the last of the money we had in the Bank of Scandinavia. We knew we would never return and it was absurd to keep the money in savings when it was so vital to us here. It was $1,805, a fortune at the time….as it would be even now. We had spent the money from my inheritance buying the land, as well as the money your father had sent us, with his limitless generosity. Our entire material, intellectual and emotional patrimony was dedicated to wildlife preservation. I have no regrets, but I feel destitute. I cannot afford to pay a competent lawyer who will revoke the sentence with a new trial. Even though I still harbor my suspicions about the intellectual authors of your murder, nothing guarantees I will ever find them. Perhaps I am only using this justification to conform to this reality because I lack the necessary funds.

My situation is not the same without you, but there are many reasons, which I have examined again and again, to stay. I have a massive task ahead of me. It is our task, which is now solely mine. I have no reason, nor any wish to return to Denmark.

Besides the economic reasons for giving up on the appeal, there are the potential consequences that may follow when this man is released from prison, which he would be at some point. I am a fragile woman, alone and in a vulnerable situation, isolated in our ranch in Cocalito. This is a small country where sooner or later we can all find each other, if we want to. It is just a question of will, the will to do good or the will to do evil.

Omar had no track record of murder, but perhaps now that he had crossed that line there would be no turning back. Killing might be easier now than it was the first time. As if this was his debut and the next action just a repetition of the first. I am convinced that this is how people become immersed in a life of crime, there is no turning back, no matter how small the crime. If eliminating an obstruction continues to be the motive, relapsing is easy, as if the first time did not count.

I suddenly noticed that I was paralyzed and shaking like a reed in a tempest. Without realizing it I had let the fear that he would harm me fester inside, and now I did not know how to stop it. How could I go from wishing I could die to panicking at the thought that he could kill me? I was becoming unbalanced, there was no doubt about it. The predator had installed himself inside my brain. I felt defeated, without the necessary strength to confront my life.

The mourning has just begun, and I don't know if it will be over before my life ends. Perhaps when I die the pain will accompany me into the grave. Despite the extension of my pain and rage, I will continue to hope that in time the people behind your murder will be discovered and justice will be served.

PART TWO

Karen and Nicolás' cabin at Cocalito.

Never forget

After the trial I decided to continue writing everything down, in case one day I was flooded by oblivion; that cruel trick played by memory of hiding things in the most unexpected places. As if our memory was a Chinese dresser with a thousand drawers, hidden in the back of a dusty attic. Perhaps it was a way to keep my sanity, trying to remember every moment and moving forward, following your instructions to fulfill your dream, our common project.

Maybe I write to keep track of passing time so that when life throws jagged blows that tear me open, I can go back to the transcript and explore all the stages of our life together. Perhaps I am searching for a balm to heal the deep wounds in my moribund soul so I can push on.

In the midst of it all, at times I feel the need to leap outside myself and seek cover in the soul of a stranger, no matter how tattered and humble it may be. It must be the soul of a stranger, unbeknownst of my wound, so it is not contaminated by the pain. But where can I find that innocent soul willing to sacrifice and accept my pain?

The world has turned since its inception, but we are unaware of the movement while living stable lives, feeling like we are perched on a perfectly stable platform. That perception changes if something shakes us violently. Suddenly, we are aware of all the threats looming above us and imagine all the ways we can die. When it feels like every swirl of air carries an omen, unequivocally sent by the oracles with our name indelibly etched in fire.

There were so many things that I did not know, because you always took care of them. Essential knowledge for conservation which is not written down in any manual and is so necessary for my survival now. It is not like I simply sat and watched you making every day viable: stroke by stroke, seed by seed, nail by nail to strengthen our existence. Our labors were divided, a life built by us both. We accomplished it together, but I don't know if I can carry on alone. Maybe I just don't want to.

I look back at my life before I met you. My fear of cancer had led me to a fortune teller. You laughed so hard the first time I told you all the details, that I could not finish because your laughter hurt me. It was, in any case, an experience I will never forget. I waited for the session to begin in a small room filled with candle laden altars, covered with images of saints and virgins. I thought I was making a mistake and nearly left. He was a young, attractive man, with big dark eyes and thick brows. He looked Hindu and wore some sort of black, lace pajama, with many buttons. I went without an appointment, but he said he had been expecting me when he opened the door. I looked at him with distrust, and made no attempt to hide it, making him aware that I was cautious of fraudsters. It would have been a contradiction for me to be there, however, if I had thought it was a fraud.

I reflected afterwards that his comment was probably a cliché, a ruse to impress the clients, a salesman strategy to obtain the desired result and by the time the session began I was back at ease. He spoke of my family's past in generalities that could apply to any person or circumstance as he shuffled his worn tarot cards and splayed them on the table. It was like the horoscopes I read with my sister Lis; we would create ridiculous headlines about the prosperity and love they predicted week after week.

I was awed, however, when he revealed a diagnosis of myxedema. "Myxedema", he said, as he looked into my eyes. It nearly made me jump out of the upholstered chair, I felt springs underneath the coarse cretonne cloth. He laid his long, warm hands on top of my cold hands and reassured me that I had been cured and there would be no relapse. I pulled my hands away and clutched them firmly on the tablecloth. I interlaced my fingers and closed myself off even more; I did not want to provide any more information. Let him earn his wage without my help, he was a fortune teller after all.

A moment later he touched two of the cards, flashing an asymmetrical smile, and announced that soon I would be married. I looked at him incredulously, as I didn't have a boyfriend and was not attracted to anyone at the time.

"With a foreigner" he said, twirling his eyes theatrically, as he opened them wide "you will live in a Latin country, surrounded by trees and horses."

I left there a little confused, not knowing how much credibility he deserved, but impressed at the mention of my past illness. The myxedema had caused me enough concerned for me to seek out Doctor Nolfi's clinic and learn about her cancer treatments. I had abandoned studying for my second degree, against my father's wishes, and had taken a job cleaning rooms at the Humlegården Rawcost Sanatorium. I wanted to see for myself what measures I could take to avoid cancer. My job cleaning rooms allowed me to investigate treatments based on consuming raw food, since the cooking process destroys many of the beneficial properties in our food.

You arrived there for the same reason. You wanted to learn the methodology of the famous doctor, who was well known beyond Denmark, as your mother and sister had both died of cancer.

We thought it was directly linked to nutrition and the contamination of the soil and water. Our beliefs were reaffirmed by my own experience with an abscess, which had grown rapidly in two weeks and had been eliminated by the iodine content of raw carrots. We were both trying to escape our fateful destiny. We were united by the idea of a simpler life, without constantly struggling to survive.

It was less than one month after my visit to the fortune teller that I met you, and you know the rest of the story. At the time, the mention of a Latin country brought to mind Spain or Italy. America did not even enter my head. As I walked out he said

"Listen carefully; if your eyes and ears are open the world will reward you."

So, I decided to keep my eyes and ears open from that day on, since it seemed like good advice. I don't know how many gifts I might have gotten before you appeared, but you were by far the best.

The memory of ghosts

As I search my memory, other ghosts appear; some are invited, others are not. I recalled a stranger that I met on a trip I had made on my own, months before your death, when you had cut the sole of your right foot and could not walk. I told you the story when I returned. I went to Carate to look for wild avocado seeds, whose fruit was beloved by Mantled Howlers and White-faced Capuchins. The gringo, self-confident and arrogant, spoke at length about his project to deforest a large stretch of Corcovado to plant citrus trees for exportation. I asked him if he could estimate the value of that forest. I spoke to him about your plans to create a reserve and our ideas about the importance of protecting primary forests for the continuous development of life. I tried to make him understand the magnitude of the loss it would represent to the resources of the planet if his project were to continue. His initial look of astonishment turned to contempt, when he realized who he was speaking with, and he abruptly moved away from me. The man was in his forties; he was tall, strong, and muscular. I noticed his large hands, covered in grooves and scars; hands which had undertaken plenty of hard work at the will of their abrasive commander.

You can't imagine how much I have wondered if that conversation had been an imprudence on my part. I was not sure of the culpability of this man, whose name I didn't even know, but the uncertainty that he may have paid to take your life ate away at my soul. I had no proof and could not accuse him, but the thought reoccurred to me infinitely that words are like jagged rocks: we cast them not knowing who they might impact or the effect they might have when they land. I reflected on our lives. Although we don't realize it, so often they hang on a thread, or "on the wings of a cockroach" as they say here. We humans are so oblivious, so insignificant, yet we are filled with limitless arrogance…Sometimes I think it is simply how we stave off panic when we recognize our vulnerability.

Here I am, back at our forest home, although I know it will not be easy. I am a widow. It is my tragedy, my open wound, and my civil state. I wish I could ignore my emotional condition, tile it over and cover it up completely. Now that I am alone, I am exposed as the small creature that I am: pure fragility. Like a delicate cup, crafted from the finest crystal and in the midst of a tempest, at risk of shattering into a million pieces with the slightest gust of wind. The revelation of my fragility terrifies me. I masticate this hardship into the marrow of my bones. Perhaps this same terror pushes me in the opposite direction, forcing me to forge the stony will to push forward, drop by drop, grain by grain. I do this for you. I will continue to breathe for the both of us, I will resist, even if I am a shadow of my former self. My current minuscule, unconscious state can only improve, as you would say of a sapling plant…

I avoid people, I don't want to see anyone. I want to ruminate my suffering in solitude, until it is digested into each one of my cells.

My pain is my own, it is not for sharing. It occupies me entirely, from the marrow of my bones to the last pore on my skin, it is my defining feature above all others. The pain ties me to you and I cannot let anything untie that knot, because if it were my choice, if I could truly decide, I would choose to leave alongside you. In the meantime, is there not a place where I can hide from the world? A place where nothing and no one can give me their hateful compassion?

Some sort of agoraphobia occupies me, which forces me to shun other people. A fear of people. A fear that they might hurt me with their well-intentioned comments, with their opinions, prying into my life and digging up my pain. I also fear a possible murderer. If they have killed you, what is to stop them from killing a depressed, fragile woman? I acquired a small caliber pistol, enough to cause a mortal wound to anyone who gets too close. It could end up being a complication, and I don't know if you would approve. It could get stolen or they might be quicker than me in reaching for it, if they ever show up at the house. But on this occasion, the weapon has chosen me, not the other way around and it is staying with me for the moment. Perhaps one day, my soul will find my lost tranquility and I will no longer need a gun. I must find a way to fight this irrational panic that won't let me breathe and suffocates me like a pair of iron hands around my throat. I keep thinking that the murderers are still on the loose, and they will come for me someday. Those who commit atrocities trust their plot will remain secret, but nobody lays silent forever, except for the dead. I keep the hope that someday the truth will come to light. I know there are more types of sadness than there are of joy, more words to describe fear than to describe bravery, more words for suffering than happiness. And so, I will have the opportunity to write a torrent of sad verses during my endless, agonic nights.

Our neighbors, John and Donna, stopped by this morning to offer their condolences. I did not want to see them, but they rapped incessantly on the bamboo at the entrance. I had no option but to let them in. John brought some cashew seeds. It was a nice gesture and I am not so stubborn as to ignore the need for allies in my despair. I could speculate to infinity and end up with my failed conspiracy theories, unable to make any progress. They offered me their help as they spoke to me softly, as if I were a child, unable to comprehend. Their eyes were glazed and emotive, it was I who could not bear to look at anybody. I want to be left alone to devour my loneliness in large, umbrageous gulps. I want to drown in a soliloquy with my sadness. I realize now that we have lived our lives isolated from the rest of world and I feel very lonely.

They told me something I did not know. About a year ago, the administrators of the company Bosques de Osa offered to sell their friends from the United States land in Corcovado so they could develop a project which would include a marina for luxury yachts.

If things had been different, and the president and Congress would have already approved the creation of the reserve on the

Osa, perhaps you would be here with me now, and I would not have written anything down in this notebook. I could not understand why the president would not approve the conservation of this area, what powerful arguments caused him to abandon the project? Who would be negatively affected by a decision to protect it? I asked them for the name of the administrator, but they claimed not to know it. They reminded me that I was a single woman facing off against a powerful, unknown enemy, as if I didn't know that already.

The letters

*I*s it possible to confront the continuity of your existence when your will opposes it? I don't have the answer. I only know that I must carry on living, even as my life hangs on a thread, dangling in the wind. I am always dressed, day and night, to hide my jagged bones. The clothes give me a ghostly aspect, like a dressed-up skeleton. I have not weighed myself, as it has no importance. I can only wear the dresses my shoulders can prop up, even if they look like the flame of a candle swollen by the wind. I don't have any skirts or pants that will stay on my body; they slide off onto the floor. I should adjust the buttons on my shirts and pants, but I don't have the energy for it. They say time heals all wounds, but how can we help time move faster? I am not yet ready to stand up and walk, I don't know if I ever will be.

My dearest Olof, although it seems pointless, life must somehow go on. I started organizing all the correspondence in different groups, the copies of the letters sent and the responses. Since I could not stop breathing, I had to learn how to breathe again, remembering the *Pranayama* technique: fill the lungs with air and empty them, rhythmically rising and falling. I smelt the humid musk on the paper and ran my fingers on the copy of the letter in which you described this country to our friends.

Searching for the remaining traces of you has become my priority. I make an inverted journey, travelling in reverse. It is the only way I can exists, flipping backwards through the calendar.

I found a pile of letters from our family and from the Speleby Group, a collective of friends we had formed for correspondence. You had asked them to form a chain of communication and mail the letters on to each other, so we could save on stamps. There was no need to send individual letters to tell the same tale. Thanks to your extreme organization there are copies of each of the letters. Reading the letters brought me back to September 1st, 1954, to those days of uncertainty in Chimaltenango, Guatemala. I was shaken as I relived the hardships that we went through, but I would go through them all one thousand times if I could have you by my side once again.

I explored the words that described our disappointments, like a broken necklace spilled over a map of the New World. I realized that the language describing the illnesses and despair is much richer than language describing health and wellbeing. Our first disappointment coincided with our first destination: Esmeraldas, Ecuador. We discovered that the interview we had read in the newspaper with the Swede who owned a banana plantation was a lie. We had believed the claims that he was living a healthy life in paradise with a fruit base diet.

The old proverb that "lies can take you anywhere but returning is impossible" is true. We had crossed the globe to reach that place. When we crossed the Panama Canal, the anxiety became unbearable, because we were so near to what we thought would be our final destination.

Esmeraldas is a province on the northern coast of Ecuador which is covered with magnificent mangrove forests growing in the estuaries, despite the salinity. It was plain to see why the Guaraní call these trees "manglar" or twisted tree. They reach great heights and provide a natural protection from hurricanes and tsunamis. These forests, where aquatic, amphibian and terrestrial creatures live in perfect harmony, are rich in biodiversity.

When we complained to the Swedish owner of the banana plantation about his deceptive interview published in the newspaper he blurted out:

"You must have less ideology and more ideas to improve the economy, that is what is needed."

But you could not hold your tongue and replied belligerently:

"Is it possible to live without ideals? Is it only worth remembering and perpetuating the history of money, with its multiple whims and guises?"

He looked at you with disgust, unable to understand our repulsion to his slavish endeavor. It was clear that place was not for us and we quickly fled.

We travelled to Honduras, although I cannot recall why we chose that country and not one closer to Ecuador. Perhaps it was so we could make our way towards Mexico, as we had read so much about that country. Honduras pained us terribly. The earth had been scorched and the life-giving humus had been gulped up by fire. Far and wide, for kilometers on end, only squalid pines and cactus could survive, along with cornfields which were planted with a long rod fitted with an iron point. The seeds were dropped in the dug-out hole and covered up; a primitive technique which appeared troglodyte at best.

We discovered the prodigious avocado, although it was not cherished there. Instead, the saplings were pulled from the earth as if they were weeds contaminating the soil. Without trees these ruined lands only produced corn, insufficient to feed a young population, in constant growth and with a lingering hunger that spanned the centuries. You described this poverty, previously unknown to us, to your father and friends in Sweden.

In Sweden there is no true misery. Since our departure from Germany, we have witnessed a nauseating misery down every road we have travelled in the New World. We have seen many possibilities to restore life, but there is only ruined land for kilometer after kilometer; cornfields, and pastures that produce next to nothing. If they had planted trees, this land could have produced an abundance of food in 10 years, but hardly anyone plants trees. When an avocado sapling emerged from the earth it was nearly always cut down. Karen and I were immensely happy when we found avocados, a fruit which one can survive on without supplementing with other foods...

In the places through which we travelled, women carried a child on each arm, another in the womb and one on their back. They would often have another child by their side who could barely walk. When living in harmony with Nature, the reproductive cycle of every organism is programmed by Nature. We don't understand every detail of how it works, but we don't need to. One thing is for certain: no animal species reproduces beyond its limits...

Reading Darwin's doctrine, written in your pointed script, I could almost hear your voice pronounce the words, as I had heard it many times before. I could see your familiar gesture: your chin resting on your hands and your gaze lost in the horizon, as if that imaginary line held all the answers that we can never find. You could hold that pose indefinitely, withdrawn in your meditations. Sometimes I felt curious and I would ask:

"What are you thinking about?"

Most of the time you would answer:

"Nothing"

I would get so upset when you replied that you were thinking about nothing!

"It is impossible to be so focused and to think about nothing", I would say. But you would just smile, fixing your gaze on the horizon once again and say:

"I am thinking about nothing, men don't need to think all the time. It is exhausting to constantly have the engine running...."

Your reply would disarm me, because I never knew if you were serious or if it was a joke to dissipate my anger.

I continue reading until I am paralyzed when I reach a reference to the children that we never had. At the time we still thought they would come someday. Frustration would overtake me when month after month that cycle that occupies and preoccupies all women came. Every month you would comfort me sweetly, with carefully chosen words that caressed my ears and calmed my spirit. In time, we decided to accept that we could not have it all and the smaller creatures of the forest came to fill that void. The arrival of little *Lis* into our lives was much like an adoption; one achieved without filling out bureaucratic paperwork and without visiting the waiting rooms of government offices. Since our journey began in Sweden, we were devoted to the observation of all the life that surrounded us, with the drive of dedicated entomologists.

Throughout this time, many things have become clear to us. We are certain that all living things in Nature are directed by waves, such as those that direct airplanes on autopilot. All the plants are full of special vibrations, even after they die, but the vibrations change. If exposed to fire, the original life form ceases to exist, but may continue to exist in another form.

When an animal feeds on the food designated by Nature, the impulses by which Nature directs its life are integrated into its body. When we humans kill the vibrations of the food that gives us nourishment with fire or when we replace the light of the sun with the light of fire or when we replace clean air with another type it is like a plane that has lost its bearings or a renegade robot, no longer under the control of its owner.

The energy of life reaches us from Space. Life which was part of our body is reborn in the organisms of the earth and transmitted to the plants which carry on living.

Our land generated much more potential before the use of fire. When we started burning the opposite occurred: the vegetation, our nourishment, and all the animals or animal products that make up our known flora and fauna lose their potential at an ever-faster rate...

The letters we sent to our friends in Europe also documented our economy of resistance in great detail. Our decision to sell our house in Speleby, our only estate, made me recall our first home with trepidation, but left me no nostalgia. It was a dry winter that year, in 1953, and it altered the agriculture with grave consequences to food production which was only beginning to stabilize after World War II to meet the needs of a growing population.

I have clear memories of March 6th when we awoke to the news of Stalin's death. It was a frigid morning. The snow from the day before had not melted and the glacial morning air cut through our skin. There was speculation among our friends and neighbors of the consequences for Finland, which shared a border with the USSR, as well as the consequences for the rest of the world. The newspapers could not fulfill the demands of a news hungry population. People of all ages arrived at the newsstands early, waiting in line with glum faces, hoping to get a paper before supply ran out. European people on both sides of the political spectrum would be shocked for differing reasons in the days to come.

Finally, the stormy, turbid, political waters receded, the echoes of World War II still booming in our ears. The effects of the war were still palpable in all of Europe; nobody wanted to remove the ashes and tear open wounds that had still not healed.

We did not write much before we reached Costa Rica. We had no good news for our families and writing back with bad news would have simply piled on our gratuitous suffering. The letter you wrote from Puntarenas one month after our arrival, however, reflected a drastic change in our lives; feeling vigorous and hopeful, despite our shortages and worries. We felt as if we had finally reached our place in the world.

In that letter, dated June 30th, 1955, you explained in great detail characteristics of the population, the weather, and the flora and fauna. Your joy was overflowing. If I didn't know the veracity of the contents of the letter, I might think you were peddling a dream. The letter is addressed to members of the Spelebykretsen with the idea that they would join us on our adventure once we were settled and create a commune.

I will attempt to describe this part of the country to give you an idea of the reason for our excitement about this land. Let's see: Costa Rica.

*Location: 10° north of the Equator.
Population density: 16 people per square kilometer.
Total population: 900,000.
Area: 51,011 square kilometers.
The following data refers to the Nicoya Peninsula, the northwestern section of the country:
Tallest mountains: 800 m.
Weather: warm and pleasant, about 25° in the shade with little variation between daytime and nighttime temperatures. With these conditions, nothing more than a sheet is needed to pass the night. In some places a mosquito net is necessary (we have spent the night in the primary forest sleeping on a bed of leaves, completely nude, without suffering any insect bites. If the forest has been burned, on the other hand, the insects tend to be very aggressive).
Rainy season: lasts six to seven months. The most precipitation falls between September and October. During this time of year, the mornings are sunny. Around two or three in the afternoon the clouds roll in, followed by torrential rain which usually lasts fifteen to thirty minutes; it is unusual for the rain to last more than an hour.
Dry season: runs from November to May. There is very little rain; the annual precipitation is about 2000 ml.
Vegetation: tropical dry forest, the trees lose their leaves in dry season. Nevertheless, there are hundreds of tree species and they lose their leaves in different ways, so the forest is never fully bare. There are at least five tree species in these forests that produce edible fruit.
Due to the intensity of the dry season, the top layer of soil dries out completely. Fire is customarily set to the forest at this time, leaving it to bellow smoke and simmer for weeks, sometimes months. Even though the fire is often limited to the understory, it*

is enough to kill the vegetation that occupies this level of the forest and the sapling trees, along with anything else living here: seeds and an endless variety of God's creatures such as insects, birds, frogs, lizards, caterpillars, snakes, deer, and other mammals...

On that very same day, when we went to the post office to mail the letter, we received a letter from Immigration with a document confirming our residency. Ecstatic, nervous and excited, you wrote the good news on the outside of the envelope: *We now have permanent residency.*

Olof, as I reflect on your description of sleeping nude on a bed of leaves in the primary forest without receiving any insect bites, with the perspective granted by the passage of time, I am sure this was not credible to the readers in Sweden. Also, the notable difference in the insect behavior in the burned forest. It only seems logical that they should be more aggressive, given the cause and effect of the aggression they received by the fire.

There are dolphins in the ocean, two to three meters long, as well as sharks. The sharks don't seem to harm anyone (they might, perhaps, if one has white skin like the belly of a fish, but that is not so common here). There are also turtles the size of a dinner table...

I laugh as I read the description of the Leatherback Turtle, "the size of a dinner table," but that is how they truly were. A gargantuan banquet could be served on that colossal spread.

I hear the bamboo rattle three times. I put away the letters and run to the hallway. Its our neighbor Nery, undoubtedly filled with good intentions, and I gesture to her that she is welcome. I would have preferred to remain cuddled up in our nest reading, but Nery is a good person and has genuine concern for me. If it weren't for her I would not eat lunch most days. The hours peel away, one after another, and my organism does not demand nourishment. But she brings me tortillas daily, still hot off the pan.

Lis

I miss you so much, Olof, my love, my companion. Dying once is nothing. Dying each day is terrible; it is like drinking a dose of poison drop by drop, spoonful by spoonful.... There is a part of me that feels great comfort in the company of animals, but the animals also miss you. For a while they continued to search for you, because they recognized you as the leader of the pack, especially *Lis*, the coati. Their instinctive search leaves me immobile. I watch them paralyzed as if somehow they might suddenly find you.

Knowing that the wild animals accept the rules of life and death better than humans is not helpful to me and brings me no comfort. I know their instinct tells them that life and death are one in the same; necessary for cycles to open and close. I cannot accept it, however, even as I repeat this to myself again and again.

I too continue to search for you, in every tree, behind every rock, even though my rational side refuses to appease me. I will continue to wake every day asking myself: "Who ordered this bloody deed? Where did they meet to pact it? What was the price set on your life? Now I know that many more crimes go unpunished compared to crimes that reach convictions, but I cannot accept this reality. The more sinister and exaggerated the crime, the less credible it seems. We cling to a reality which is framed by our fears. We are pacified by the idea that a tragic event cannot be as bizarre as it seems, that it must be the reality of its author written to fulfill his fantasy. The list of impunity on the planet is so long and wide, however, that one crime more or one crime less will not modify the gears of justice.

The days tumble, bit by bit, one after the other. One day buries the next with a numbing sluggishness that in turn buries our emotions, so that, thankfully, we cannot feel. Before we know it, time changes us, but it does not change the image of the departed. You, for example, will never grow old in my memory. You will remain resplendent in my memory, even as the years drag on and my skin wrinkles like a parched, flattened fig. There is a painful chasm between the real alterations we undergo and the memories that we cherish. Memories are sedentary, while life rambles on, vagrantly, right up to its last breath.

Lis went in and out of the house a thousand times searching for you and I don't know if she understood when I sat down with her to explain that you would not be coming back. She looked at me attentively, with her round eyes. She went outside when she saw my tears and returned with a banana for me, presenting it delicately in an attempt to cheer me up. You must recall her habit of bringing us things or taking them away to cheer us up and make us laugh. She no longer hides my balls of yarn, as I don't have anything to sew.

I wish our lives could be mended and lived out with a higher consciousness, sensing every stitch on our scars like the residue of a previous existence. A war wound to make us value that we lived to tell the tale.

You and I shared so many experiences with the coati. When you went out on your explorations, at the crack of dawn, I knew I would have an anecdote for you when you returned, like a playful girl who came home from school with something new each day. Remember the nest she built with leaves and sticks in the wooden beams of our ranch, with an ocean view? It was one month before she gave birth to five precious kits. I was so curious as to how she had built it, that one day I climbed up to observe it. I was apprehensive, because mothers are wary of any presence near their babies, but she was so happy, as if I was her mother coming to visit. Oh, what a celebration the three of us had that day!

It was a terrible anguish the day she came to me in a panic. After months of sharing a home with her, I immediately knew something was wrong with her kits. The images are etched in my mind and on my retina as sharply as if it had been yesterday.

You and I were picking papayas and she came to fetch us, puffing like a steam engine. At my urging, you checked the nest and found the boa. You took it by the tail and shook it with the energy of a Titan, to prevent it from eating all the kits. You didn't even consider the reaction the boa might have. You were two colossi, interacting as equals, garnering mutual respect.

Sadly, not a single kit survived, and the boa slithered slinkingly into the forest. It returned a few days later, on a routine visit, as if nothing more than an unimportant family spat had occurred.

The way you tried to save the kits impressed *Lis* and from that moment on she saw you as an omnipotent god and never left your side. I was no longer her favorite; I was relegated to second tier for everything. Even when going to sleep, she laid at your side of the bed. You were the leader of our pack, our hero. We both knew that with certainty.

The boa also knew it. It had startled me when it first came to the house, when it was still not full grown. You, however, always treated animals on equal terms, and they accepted you from the start.

Lis had another litter sometime later, and she brought them to the nest. She would leave their side only when necessary; she had learned. One day when they were old enough to learn she took them into the forest. They formed a line as they walked, and she would turn from time to time to make sure none of them strayed. She was like a kindergarten teacher, taking her students on a field trip. We would melt in tenderness watching her, like lovestruck grandparents.

Do you remember that night when *Lis* came home reeking of skunk? Her kits cried desperately. We didn't realize what was happening and *Lis* didn't either. I thought that if I could calm the mother, her litter would calm down as well. I offered her a drink of water with honey, but when she returned to the nest her young cried louder still and *Lis* seemed distressed. Then I remembered how much she liked scented talcum and I cloaked her with it. The talcum absorbed the oils in the skunk spray and we all slept soundly that night. We learned so much with the animals; they share the most valuable life lessons.

When the workers dug holes to plant trees, they frequently found all types of snakes, including Central American Rattlesnakes and Fer-de-lance Pit Vipers. They would always call you, if you were not working with them, because you had urged them to respect the life of the animals living on our property. They were always awestruck by the skill with which you delicately collected them and relocated them away from the work area.

They were also amazed at how during breaks from work the Black Spiny-tailed Iguanas would climb up your legs to eat bits of banana when you called them: "Venga garrobito." They would tamely climb up your long legs and lay on your lap, as if it were the lap of a loving mother. Your tenderness with animals was touching, considering how demanding you were with humans. Above all else, that was the most difficult thing for the workers to understand. They may have thought you disdained them, or you thought they were inferior. Those built-up feelings can induce any man to seek vengeance, so as to restore a perceived lost honor.

The workers admired how well you were organized, although they thought it too strict that you demanded the trees be planted with the exact amount of fertilizer placed at their base. You would bring your roman scale and weigh out exactly 30 pounds of fertilizer, the amount you considered optimum for the development of each tree. Also, they could not understand why you dedicated the fruit from some of the trees in the orchard exclusively for the animals to feed on. When a new worker was hired, you explained the rules of the job. Apart from their salary, they were allowed five mangoes per week. The remainder of the mangoes were left for the animals of the forest. Some of them thought this to be foolish and when you caught them eating extra mangoes you fired them on the spot. It was your way of maintaining order.

When our beehives began to produce, we would give them one bottle of honey per week, that is if they had worked five consecutive days. There was much absenteeism and the honey was an important incentive for them. Any excuse was a good one to miss work, especially when they were hungover after a night of drinking.

You would practice throwing the butterfly knife you brought from the army into a Monkey Comb Tree that was behind the house and they admired your knife-throwing skills. But there was one anecdote they always recalled fondly. One day, when there was an especially high tide, the waves stranded a Hawksbill Sea Turtle on the rocks. Our friend Frank was working when he saw the turtle struggling to return to the water and he came to fetch you. He was so impressed by the way you wrapped your arms around its shell and carried it to the shore, that he recounted your feat to everyone in town.

Your relationship with animals was both admirable and incomprehensible to our workers and neighbors. At first, they thought us extravagant, vagabonds, as they would refer to anyone that did not fit their traditions or existential views. With time, they began to know us and accept us, although they never understood us.

It is possible that these resentments, pent up in the souls of our neighbors, have begun to shine through. Feelings will explode like time bombs if they are not vented. No one enjoys feeling humiliated and undervalued. The cause of your death was not the work of an idiot or a madman. I am more convinced every day that it was a pact which was hatched to cleanse somebody's trampled self-esteem. Perhaps it was because of the expropriations or because of your deferent treatment of animals, but neither reason justifies your death. You only defended life; the life in the forest and that of our neighbors, even if they could not see it.

The children still knock on the bamboo three times when they pass by our entrance, Olof, as we asked them to do and was now customary. They still come for the fruit you always had for them. Today they approached timidly and bright eyed, with their white school shirts and their backpacks. The two older ones greeted me with a solemn "Good morning." They are so tender, so endearing. It required a titanic effort for me to tell them that I would give them fruit from now on because Don Nicolás was no longer here, but they already knew that...

Perhaps it will be easier for me to start socializing again with children, as Nery suggested. She knows about that well, as she has a marimba of 12 children, born one after another. But despite having such a numerous family, she always brings a pile of fresh tortillas, still warm from the fire. She is like an affectionate and vigilant sister, traveling the trails between her house and mine with small, quick paces, like a little elf in the forest. Sometimes she tells me about her hardships, her physical and emotional pain. Mostly she voices concerns about what will become of her children when they grow up. I feel like she does it so I can see that she also suffers, but I can't help measuring and comparing each of her sorrows and trying to determine if her burden is greater than mine. I have learned to tread cautiously with other people's sorrows to avoid absorbing them into my own. My own sorrows constitute an unbearable burden, but they belong to me.

This is a rural country with a young population. Families have children one after another, year after year. They don't consider if they have the proper conditions to bring them into this world, not the space in their homes nor the abundance or lack of food.

In October 1956 the celebrations for the birth of the one millionth baby, who received all kinds of gifts, drew our attention. Everyone from the media to local businesses raced to present the baby with gift baskets. We saw the announcement on the cover of *La Nación* during a shopping trip to San José. The newborn was a boy born in Cartago and he was the object of the country's attention because of the absurd fact that his birth coincided with a number.

Our thoughts coincided with Malthus, who considered that excessive, uncontrolled human fertility would soon exceed the available resources: *Populations always tend to increase in geometric progression, while the means of subsistence increase in arithmetic progression. Population growth is then limited through shortage of subsistence.* We had confirmed this theory in every country we traveled through on our way to Costa Rica.

Lis, the coati

Images and memories

I have found many photographs of us in the letters and I decided to organize them, noting on the back the date and place where they were taken. It is so easy to forget dates and details, especially if you never share them with anyone. Our fickle and capricious memory sets traps for us, making us believe in fabricated realities.

The first photograph is the studio shot, taken a few months before we left Sweden. Your father wanted a keepsake upon our departure. We knew that this small act would please him as he suffered so much when we talked about our travel plans. His face would darken, as if night had suddenly befallen him. It was November 1953 and the cold had not yet paralyzed us. I remember I wore my coat, which I removed for the photo, a woolen jersey, and boots. You looked as handsome as I remembered, but so serious. You were never comfortable posing for photographs.

All the other photos that I found were from the New World. The New World, that is what it was for us. Most photos were taken here, on our farm. We were so young and had so much enthusiasm for life, as if it began anew every morning.

You were showering in one photo, the water falling from an eave you had just installed. It was the first thing we did, because we could not plant without water. Those days were exhausting, but gratifying. It was a blessing to have water. Treacherously, I took the photograph without telling you. You hated posing for photographs here even more than in Europe.

Here's a photo of me washing dishes with the water that falls from the eave. You took it that same day, before you got in the shower. I took the photo of you showering in revenge, because I didn't want to be photographed either. I am so grateful to have the pictures now. The photographs will preserve in my mind how our life was, without the treacherous erosion of memory.

I found a photograph that I had completely forgotten about. It depicts a beautiful, massive owl with its wings cupped and with an opossum in its talons. It's a spectacular photo, because of the moment it captures and because of the intelligent gaze of the owl. It seems to ponder what to do in that instant, whether to drop its prey and save its own life or to try to keep both. I don't know the ending to that story and I am curious as to who took that magnificent photograph and why I had not seen it before. Could it be I am selecting which memories to keep in this process of detachment? Although I know that memories are never lost, we store them until we need them, and they resurface when we drift into daydreams or at night in our dreams.

That is how our minds work, as Carl Jung assured us. I remember your incredulous gaze when I talked to you about my lectures on the research into consciousness and unconsciousness. The study was based on archetypes and research on collective unconsciousness. I would read it in fascination, looking up from the book only to reflect on what I had read. You were so much more grounded, your beliefs and philosophies of life were based on the behavior of the wildlife that surrounded us. "It is the reality that stands before our eyes, although most humans refuse to see it..." you would say, with absolute confidence. There is so much reality in our dreams, however, and how tenuous is the balance that upholds what we consider to be our most established values. I need only to glance backwards to ascertain how my life has changed, with my most secure and solid valor dissolving from one day to the next. Feelings and beliefs make us think that there is no more certainty than our own and that is where we settle, refusing to give up those beliefs that something or someone has put into our mind. Now my life is nothing but uncertainty. I wonder day after day what dastardly character decided that you had to die to satisfy his worthless existence.

I flip to the next photo and I can see the landscape from the hilltop and the sinuous strip of white foam that draws the boundary between the land and the sea. We felt powerful up on the hill, about to own a piece of paradise. I remember we took several photos that day. We wanted to see the perspective before buying. The part of the property near the beach was completely deforested and as we made our way up the hill, we decided to buy the upper part as well, which was partly covered with vegetation and a few trees. Once we owned the land, we planted and planted trees, as if it could never be enough. We knew that with the food more and more creatures would come to live near the "pantry." Yes, animals breed when there is abundance, but refrain from breeding in scarcity.

The next photograph shows us sitting on a tree trunk, with our hats in hand. You had grown a red beard that tickled my face and you had your hair tied back at the nape of your neck. My hair was loose and with bangs, just like a little girl. The picture was taken by Manuel Muñoz, at the bottom of the hill. You had to carefully explain to him how to take the photo, because he had never held such a device in his hands, and he was afraid of doing something that would damage it. We decided to take it where we would later build the house, so we could remember how it was before and what it would be like after. We used the space that they had already cut. We didn't cut anything; we planted as many trees as we could possibly fit in our forest. How happy we were, with the tragedy that awaited us never crossing our minds. I know there are more photos from that day, amongst the messy pile, but that's enough of wallowing in the past for today. I must try to detach from that which will never return. But how…?

I am forced to return to the present. They say that there is more time than life, but it is time that leaves its mark on us. I look at my hands, with bulging veins and markings; markings which I also find on my body and face. I can't help but compare it to the photos I just saw. My hair has bleached in the months since your passing. They say that anguish and suffering can accelerate the reduction of melanin in the scalp, which appears to be true in my case. One morning, about one month after your disappearance, I discovered that my temples were white while combing my hair in front of the mirror. Just like that, from one day to the next. And little by little my head turns the color of snow, with a few gray strands. This is me, what I've become. Neither tall nor short, neither young nor old, not quite alive, but not dead either. An ordinary woman, with nothing to highlight.

There is a letter dated April 14, 1971, from your father in which he acknowledges receipt of a letter you had previously sent him. In the letter he announces that he sent a check for $1,805, which was all the savings we had in the Bank of Scandinavia after we had sold our house. We needed the money and we had asked him to send it to us in US dollars, but it had been difficult for him to write the check and he complained about it.

He also tells us about the development of skin cancer on his nose and about the treatment. He too was convinced that meat-based diets caused cancer. It is so endearing to read in his farewell: *Affectionate greetings from your old father*. Yes, he didn't have much longer to live. You didn't either, but we couldn't even imagine that.

It was precisely during that time that we drew up our will in favor of the World Wildlife Fund in case we both died together. Those days we went everywhere together and many of those trips were in small planes of dubious reliability, not to mention the lack of safety on the landing strips.

We rarely travelled alone unless it was a short trip lasting less than one day. We slept separately only a handful of times, except when you contracted malaria. You didn't want to have me around due to doubts about the diagnosis and fear of contagion. When malaria was confirmed, we felt a contradiction: on the one hand, we knew what it was and we eliminated the fear of contagion. But we knew the effects and the high risk for those who contract it. You were so weakened that I feared for your life. The recovery was slow and sometimes we doubted you were recovering at all. One day it seemed that the fever lowered, only to return the next day reinforced. I never washed so many sheets, the clothes lines were always full. The first day that you broke free from the fever, we did not know if it would be definitive; we glance at each other timidly, observing our reactions, not daring to believe that the fever had subsided. Your eyes suffered after-effects. You always thought it was because of the medications, not because of the disease, but the cause did not matter. I'm not sure now if it was late '57 or early '58.

We were grateful for the breeze that blew from the hills to the sea which alleviated your fever. At the time we only had the first lot, which we bought from Manuel Muñoz. We were planting trees and building beehives. Our apiary would eventually include two hundred hives. They were tasks that would pay off in the future, but at that moment they only meant work and more work. It was a dark tunnel with no end in sight, without the hope that one day it would end. That is how I remember those times. But the first day you walked out of the house and sat in the corridor, weak but without fever, it seemed to me that spring had come, although that season is not known here. I was so happy that I performed a version of the *Swan Lake* dance just for you, drifting through the courtyard between the two little houses. I recall your mouth was smiling, but your gaze was sad. I was tired when I finished, because the day was coming to an end and it had been a hard day, as all those days were. But I felt excited and happy to see you coming back to life.

In a letter dated January 9, 1969, you tell your father that we don't have time to write because it's time to work with the bees, since the laurels are in bloom and that's when they produce the most. *Such is the life of a beekeeper*, you tell him. You tell him how we have suffered with the fires started by some of the local farmers and all our trials working to preserve our forest from intentional burning. It was after more than 10 hectares of young mahogany, cocobolo and ron-ron trees burned. All majestic trees with precious wood.

I have built two cabins with palm leaves which are my observatories. In town I tell them that I am always sitting in one of them, watching with my rifle, so that no one sees me go in or out. Having two, they never know which one I'm in...

The trails to the cabin are hidden. Now I never walk up the hilltops, but behind them. I also put shiny objects in the cabins, so they think it's the refection of a rifle or binoculars. That's how I managed to identify the arsonist. Since the beginning of the year, he has not come within 100 meters of my property...

To our neighbors it seemed normal that the forest should burn for days on end, without doing anything to stop the fire. They were not aware that fire takes away life, that the forest would never be the same again. Thinking back, I realize that we were fighting on too many fronts, accumulating more battles without even realizing it, one by one. Here people don't confront each other directly, but whoever challenges or offends them is made to pay, sometimes with their life, as we would learn.

At times I wanted to make a list of possible murderers and the reasons they wanted you dead, but there are so many that could I never finish. The people expropriated from El Peñón alone are many, due to the large number of families in the area and the inbreeding that caused braided kinships that linked everyone to everyone. The many park rangers that were snubbed, the feverish gold miners, that man I met on the boat who wanted to plant citrus trees. Then there are the loggers from Corcovado, some of whom used to live in El Peñón and if they spared you the first time, they might not have spared a second attempted eviction… who knows! What about those companies that intend to develop tourism, which do I choose first? And who's next? Which one of them made the decision to seek out the assassin who would end your life? I don't have the strength to face your assassins, even as I am martyred by my impotence or my cowardice as I bury the days.

Puntarenas

1977

*M*y dearest Olof, I couldn't come to visit you all week. It is so difficult for one person to run the farm! We have a lot of fruit to pick and eat, but I need someone to help me with the daily chores. Despite my complete dedication, it is not possible to survive on the money that is left over after paying the laborer's salary and taxes to the municipality, even with our simple lifestyle.

You know as well as I do, because I have been telling you and because I am sure that you are watching over me from some other dimension, that it was a tenacious struggle this last year, but I cannot do it anymore. I have reached the limit of my resistance. Each one of the words I write hurts me, as if each was torn from my entrails, when I tell you that I am going to live in Puntarenas.

I am going there with an idea for a new project which will make me self-sufficient with less effort, since I am not so young anymore. I will come to Cocalito whenever I can, to check on everything and to visit you up on your hill with that view of the sea caressing Playa Colorada. I am not abandoning you, although it feels that way to me. You will be with me every moment of every hour and I will continue writing for you, so I don't forget to tell you everything when I return to visit, and I will return to stay forever someday.

I know that *Lis* the coati will miss me the most; I will miss her too as well as her antics. Her company has helped me immensely to cope with my sadness. I envy that intrinsic, natural happiness that wild animals enjoy. Their senses are more acute. Everything they perceive is more intense and they don't have to hide what they feel or pretend to be something they are not. No one criticizes them for what they do or don't do, and they are not accountable to anyone. I envy them intensely.

When packing my luggage, I find the folder labeled: *Correspondence* and I can't resist its lure. Just as I never tire of looking at your photos again and again, I pick up a letter to find you hidden in the text. This one is addressed to your father and dated January 12, 1961. As I read, I remember how you had gone to explore the tip of El Cabo, so determined. You arrived at the Víquez family house on December 28, and you returned home on Saint Sylvester's day, the last day of 1960. They treated you with extreme kindness, invited you to dinner and to spend the night, and even lent you the horse for the next day's ride. For us it was a day like any other. One more on the calendar, with nothing special to celebrate. We didn't live by anyone's standards but by our own. If you live according to the rules of others, you live anyone's life but your own.

I recalled the tension that took over your entire body when you told me how you crossed the Pánica River, pulling the reins on the frightened horse that strangely couldn't swim. I never imagined a horse that could not swim. I wouldn't have believed it if anyone but you were telling me the story. You were my hero and that day probably his hero too.

You finally arrived at that heap of piled stones, El Peñón, where José Rodríguez lived. You detailed the names of all the trees that you came across on your journey along the banks of the river. You always wanted to know everything, and you wrote it down carefully, so that nothing would get lost. You wanted to know the truth to the deepest core, the vital essence of all beings. You didn't realize that there is a different reality in every mind that does not exist anywhere else; only there. But all your empathy was directed towards the wildlife. You had no interest in relationships with human beings, whom you severely judged for their irresponsibility and lack of compassion towards other living beings. Perhaps for them you were just a hindrance that obstructed their purposes, an annoying bug that had to be exterminated, even though they treated you cordially.

In the letter you assure your father that no one in the world is as happy as we are and that we would not trade our lives for any other. It was the greatest truth. There was no money in the world capable of buying our happiness. Knowing that this was our place in the world, our Paradise, and feeling immensely lucky to have found it.

Today I feel such deep gratitude towards these letters, as if they were relatives that I could visit to feel you, with whom I can talk to about you. Your hand and your thoughts are printed on these sheets of paper, which would be soulless without your intervention. A derivative of cellulose whose manufacture devastates the forests. I will take them all with me, to accompany my loneliness in Puntarenas. They will also help me in moments of discouragement, when I believe that the problems that afflict me have no solution. They will help me relive those moments in which life seemed to stop us from moving forward. When it slowed us down, like the meanders of a river stop it from flowing, until the next day it finds its way forward once again. These letters will give me hope to move forward.

A letter sent to your father on July 4, 1971, slips out of the folder as I close it. In the letter you give him details of the Japanese cargo and passenger ship, *The Great Ranger*, which sank in the Balsitas area three weeks before. I clearly remember the sound of the ship's siren that day because it is lodged in a part of my brain linked to our departure from Sweden. The noise broke like thunder in the middle of that calm and bright July afternoon. There were three whistles in a row, repeated over half an hour in a relentless request for help.

We were checking the fences before dark so that the cows would not invade our forest. Hearing the crash, we shot each other looks ranging somewhere between fear and astonishment, as if the sound were a sign of the apocalypse. We understood that someone out at sea was asking for help. We rushed back as fast as we could. You were patrolling with your rifle and we dropped it off in the house before taking the road to Montezuma to find out what had happened. The entire town was in an uproar. Everyone marched by boat, on horseback, and by oxcart towards the tip of El Cabo, on Playa Balsitas, as it was the closest point to the shipwreck. No one had never seen a ship this size so close to shore.

We learned later that most of the passengers and crew had abandoned the ship and swam to the coast, helped by those who responded to the distress call. Our neighbors from the town of Mal País, who were in the area responded to the emergency signal, but little by little, people also arrived from Santa Teresa, San Isidro, Cabuya, and Montezuma. Curiosity has a powerful call; especially in these towns where nothing relevant ever happens, or so it seems.

The ship's cargo constituted of four hundred and thirty Toyota cars, and an endless number of household goods, furniture, and food; all jealously stored in the ship's cargo hold. In the following days, many of the canned food floated to the beach, like a manna that delighted our neighbors, whose main activity became fishing for all kinds of junk that sailed through the hole in the ship's hull. Hundreds of things that they had never seen or even imagined: special pots for cooking, frying pans, boxes of canned ham and other sausages, chairs, mirrors, perfumes, watches...

All the local inhabitants looked for a way to get closer to the ship. Sometimes at night small lights could be seen in the area. Everyone knew that looting had begun and would continue until all stocks were depleted. Despite the fact that the Government installed a guard to prevent robberies, little or nothing could be done when the scope of the ocean is so vast. It was like attempting to put doors on the forest, or on the ocean, in this case.

On the other hand, it was a tragedy that all the cargo would be laid to waste. Naturally, there was no way to get the cars out, due to the risk that the ship would sink during the maneuvers, but other minor things could be saved. The worst thing they brought, in my opinion, were televisions. It was the first breakthrough of the appliance that families valued the most. It would become everyone's favorite a short time later, when electricity arrived, and the television was given a space of honor in their homes.

We found out later that during those days these towns saw the most excessive debauchery in their history, due to the nocturnal visits of some treacherous assailants who boated out to the ship and ventured on board to loot boxes of whiskey, fine wines, and all kinds of spirits of every origin. Don Walter Ledezma, from Santa Teresa, told the story of a neighbor who stayed on the ship for three days. It is not clear whether he was unable to stand or if he stayed to protect his treasure until it was completely consumed. At his house they thought he was dead, and they were arranging to pay for religious services dedicated to his soul when he reappeared, with his eyes lit up like light bulbs and his body and clothes manifesting the absence of soap and water. The kids fled when they saw him, thinking it was his ghost.

I have heard that since the captain was not on the ship, the property inside is considered abandoned. Apparently, in this case the captain was not the last to leave, so he lost ownership of the ship and its contents. Thinking back, with the coldness granted by time elapsed, it was very strange to have an accident of such magnitude, on a clear day and in broad daylight, with full view of the rocks and all their contours. Weeks later rumors circulated that it was an intentional act to collect on a massive insurance policy, the size of the unpronounceable amounts left everyone speculating. We never found out how it was resolved; nor did we care about matters that did not concern our wildlife.

In the letter, you also tell your father how excited we were at the possibility of expanding the Reserve. We awaited the response from the International Union for the Conservation of Nature (IUCN). It was an arduous task to re-negotiate the purchase of land, but also a confirmation that we were on the right track towards wildlife restoration.

You explain to your father that you did not recover full mobility in your right hand after the lateral paralysis you suffered a year after arriving in Costa Rica. That was another setback we had to overcome. You wrote with two fingers of your left hand and your handwriting was at first illegible. During that time, we had little contact with family and friends as we didn't want to worry them. One day you decided that you had another hand and you would use it. Although you were very demanding and you were never satisfied with the results, little by little your handwriting improved. It wasn't the same as with the right hand, but nearly so. "Accepting our own limits makes us grow", you said after the third attempt and the first letter sent written with the erratic hand, as you called it.

One year after the Great Ranger we received the news of your father's death. It was unexpected. We found out in a letter from

Ulla and Sven sent in June that he was going to have surgery to remove a gallstone. The operation went well, but the postoperative period was complicated, and he died on July 7. A very brief letter from Bjorn said that he was already resting in peace, in the family vault in Vrigstad; a very sad day for us indeed.

English and Yoga classes

I am, here in Puntarenas, in a corner house on the north side and in front of the church. Elisa Cascante told me that the church was built in honor of the Virgen del Carmen, the maritime Madonna. It is a mortar and stone structure with unique architecture; I haven't seen any other church with such features. Inside, some of the columns display the devotion and generosity of some of the wealthiest families. It has a clock on the bell tower, so I won't need to look at the time anymore, because I hear it ring out at all hours of the day. In Cocalito we had the sundial that you had engraved on the cement slab, between the two cabins, and here I have the one on the bell tower. Indeed, I will not be needing a wristwatch. Between the house and the church there is a garden with trees and some benches where I can sit when I feel the walls closing in on me.

Behind the house there is a boulevard with sculptures, marking the entrance to the House of Culture, which was only inaugurated two months ago. The building previously housed the Navy Command. It looks more like a barracks than anything else, but I think that's the best use for an old military building. You see, I will have plenty of entertainment between the church and the House of Culture.

The zinc on the roof of the house is very rusty because of the salinity and its proximity to the Pacific. It is a little house painted in light blue, with a small corridor, a door that is narrower than the standard door, and a window on each side. That's how they build here: without standards. First, they make the walls of the house and the hole between the walls is the door. Then, they make each door to the size of each of the remaining holes. The same procedure is followed with the windows. It is large and spacious, with a large living room and two bedrooms. The kitchen is located towards the backyard, where the grass grows wild, without anyone tending to it. There are some burners and a sink on the back wall, the backyard wall. Opposite the kitchen is the toilet. I have more than enough space to live.

I put a sign up for the yoga school and the English school this morning and my first student enrolled today. Her name is Isabel.

The method I follow is Richard Hittleman's *Yoga for Health*. He has a television series in England and has published a book with the same title. I got the book through Ruth and Ben, from California, because there is no way to buy it here. It is edited in London. Following the guidelines, I have practiced daily for three months. You know how dedicated I am when something interests me, and yoga brings me the great inner peace that I have been yearning. Richard's technique begins with the most basic postures of *Hata Yoga* and progresses little by little. It is an easy plan, so beginners can follow it without difficulty. The most important thing is to feel good with the practice, perfecting the asanas is not essential.

I feel very hopeful, which is something I haven't felt since you have been gone. I am not sure if that feeling of the lightness in the air is worthy of a grieving widow. Even if you can't manifest yourself, I know you wouldn't want me to live my life perpetually looking backwards to that time when we were two. You and I never encouraged victimhood and I have learned that death is not sad. The sad thing is not knowing how to live.

After your death, I carried on because of the moral obligation that we acquired when we came into the world to live the life that others, including you, have not been able to live. Also, because of our commitment to the wildlife and the forest. But now that little tingle that the yoga school gives me is very, very pleasant. It makes me feel more alive. I think I can be happy again, in another way. I will bloom again, even if spring has passed.

It is the third night since I arrived here. The first night I heard noises in the corridor, but I was prudent and did not go out. I know the behavior of animals, but human beings are unpredictable and sometimes fear overtakes me in an irrational way. When I opened the door in the morning, there was a kitten in a cardboard box. She was only a few weeks old and was faint from hunger. She didn't even meow. I put some milk in a saucer and in no time at all she was rubbing on my feet and scratching my flip-flops. I'm not alone anymore.

Before deciding on a name, I checked to see if it was male or female. I have named her *Mis*, she is tabby, with honey-colored eyes and she grows day by day. I inquired with my neighbors before adopting her, but no one claimed her or knew how she got here, so this cutie and I are family now.

My dear love, I've been here almost a month. The yoga school has some ten students already, and the English school has a few more. Thanks to them I think I will be able to meet my economic goal; to earn a living from my classes and pay the taxes on the farm. I alternate them on the days of the week. Three days yoga and another three English. This is a pleasant life, despite the sticky heat, the smells of salting fish from the estuary, and the fuel of the engines that emanate from the port. What I miss the most are the animals in our forest. My White-nosed Coatis, the howls of the Mantled Howlers and my life surrounded by nature. I have learned to live in a different way, however, and as you said, "A person committed to a cause is not distracted; his time is always productive and there are no empty spaces between the discourse of his conscience and his daily chores". In my case it's still like that. That's why I've been able to adapt without too much difficulty here. Now I am certain that there is more than one alternative to move forward. Fortunately, death cannot be willed no matter how much I had wished for it.

After your death I entered a pernicious state of apathy from which I am slowly emerging. I feel like balance has returned to me. I can feel it through my movements, which have been more relaxed, and I feel it every morning when I stretch during yoga before receiving my students. While the air moves slowly, in and out of my lungs, practicing *pranayama*, I feel the presence of the primitive atom and the immensity of the cosmos navigate through each of my cells. I think it must be similar to the feeling of fullness. I don't know if I can call it happiness, because that is still a nebulous feeling for me, but I thank the Universe every day for living in this beautiful place and giving me the faculties to take care of myself. Perhaps happiness has different shapes that we are not capable of evaluating. Could it be the coherence each one of us has within?

I feel *"das Einfühlungsvermögen"* surfing in me, you know, that empathy that fuses me with my surroundings. It makes me believe that I am part of something indivisible and that this inseparable whole has plans for me that I don't even realize.

You see, yoga feels something like levitation. You may think that I am exaggerating, but I tell you that practicing yoga allows me to ruminate things with a certain distance and benevolence to others and to myself: forgive them and forgive me. But the most important thing about yoga is breathing and stretching. That allows the energy to travel through our anatomy and connect us with the vibration of the earth. The experts say that this vibration is increasing year after year, and it is difficult for living beings to adapt to the new rhythm and to balance ourselves with its pulse. I repeat this to my students daily. The animals know it, no one needs to tell them.

Puntarenas is growing and seems unrecognizable as the days go by. There are more and more hotels, and more tourism, and each month the number of my students grows, especially in the English classes. I don't have room for more. Only women of all ages come to yoga classes. At first it was only foreigners, but now there are also Costa Ricans. One of them is Isabel, and it turns out she is the girl who told me about your photo in the newspaper, the day I went looking for you. I didn't recognize her, when she came to register the first day, but when she arrived for class she identified herself. She is the first to pay every month. She knows…

Another student is Georgina, a beautiful Italian, with three children who are as beautiful as she is. They live nearby, a block from home. Today she told me that her oldest, Eduardo, will sign up for English classes. The boy has an intelligent and curious look. He told me that he will be a ship captain when he grows up, like Marco Polo. I understand that having Italian ancestors, Marco Polo is an ideal adventurer and a perfect model for someone dreaming of a life full of great deeds. What child has not had that desire, right?

Oh, I must tell you that our family has also increased. I have two more kittens that were left at my door the other morning. I don't know if I'll have to put up a sign up saying "our family is full", so that they don't leave me any more kittens. They are two females and I named them Cris and Susi. This house is intense and exquisitely feminine. I'm going to sleep, weariness always gets the best of me at this hour.

Dear Olof, I haven't written to you since I returned from my last trip to our house. You know that writing makes me feel like I am communicating with you and it comforts me. I think I write more for myself than for you, but in any case, I need to do it.

I told you during my visit, filled with emotion and with a lively, tremulous voice, my surprise at how very beautiful everything was. All the vegetation was green and shiny after the first rains, as if it was newly born. Wrapping my feet in the soil and feeling the whispering trees shake their leaves to greet me as I hugged them was a delirious experience. Of course, *Lis* showed up right away and she wouldn't let me move, surrounding me so that I had to listen to her scold me for my long absence.

I toured the reserve, our beautiful dream come true, with Carlos, the park ranger. It still seems incredible to me that we managed to create the first nature reserve in Costa Rica, thus initiating the System of Reserves and National Parks. But at that time the task was in its infancy. The appointment of park rangers to protect the reserve clashed with a lack of rigor in the performance of their duties. You observed them in secret. As a consequence, several of them were dismissed for non-compliance. Allowing hunting, planting beans, or cutting down trees were some of the misdeeds. The most serious offence, perpetrated by a very conflictive policeman, was to kill and eat the last Central American Spider Monkey in the reserve. Furious, you rushed to the office of the Institute of Lands and Colonization in San José to demand his immediate dismissal and exemplary punishment. The reluctance to dismiss the offender was interpreted by you as a symptom of corruption of those responsible for the Institute of Lands and Colonization, as you wrote in the letters sent to your father. You were so visceral. They were officially bound by a procedure that they had to follow. Your sentence was not enough.

Later, this fired park ranger denounced you on Radio Puntarenas as a horse thief, who threatened the owners at gunpoint to steal them. The San José police arrived to arrest you, but you explained to them that you had paid the owners for their horses. The policemen were surprised when you confessed that up to date you had not killed one, but one hundred and eighty horses, although you assured them that you had purchased them all beforehand. They questioned your motives, and you replied that you were sacrificing them so that they did not have to suffer in their pitiful state. You did not tell them that before their death you gave them a good meal and that when you buried them you planted a tree on their grave so that they would continue to give life, perpetuating the life/death/life cycle that governs our ecosystem. We never found out if the announcer of the Radio Puntarenas corrected the details of the news after the clarification. A rectification was not sensationalist, and nobody would pay attention to that extravagance. And although they did not understand your point of view, they could not arrest you, because there was no crime.

Finally, the ITCO and the Philadelphia Conservationists reached an agreement about surveillance: you would select the park rangers for the Reserve.

We created a questionnaire about plants and animals to test their knowledge and to aid in the selection process. You inserted questions to trip them up, to hear how they would handle a possible bribe from hunters. Back then people were very innocent and sometimes naive. They did not know how to cheat. You would ask what they would do if they were offered money to allow the hunt of a puma, some answered that it would be necessary to get more details on the offer. They had not understood anything about the function for which they would be hired and paid.

I have tried and succeeded to forget them, and I can't remember the names of any of the guards who passed through here until Carlos arrived. His arrival marked a new chapter.

While walking with Carlos I thought about how lucky we were to get him to stay on as a guard. He is the best park ranger we could have found; he loves wildlife, like we do, and defends it with courage and dignity, without wasting a minute of his time or effort. He has a good partner, Miriam, who helps him with his tasks, sharing responsibilities without limits or divisions. They live there with only the basic commodities, with their two girls and a boy. A ranch without walls and three stones for a stove. I have never heard them complain about their work or their life. They fulfill their tasks above and beyond what is expected of them, despite the risks of confronting hunters and fishermen and without the resources to pursue them. They risk their lives daily, just like you and I did. Others will be decorated on big stages, with medals pinned to their puffed-out chests. To add insult to injury, we will have to read and listen to false and hollow statements in the press that justify and magnify their valiant efforts. Sitting in international offices, responsible for achieving this and that and the other. But none of them have been drenched in a downpour, burned in the sun, shattered their feet walking through the woods of the reserves, or felt fear for their lives while chasing down poachers. That part corresponds to the park rangers. Some do the work and others collect the glory, that is just how it is.

I told Carlos of my regret for not having accompanied you on that trip to Corcovado. It is something so feminine, something so characteristic of women, to give priority to domestic tasks instead of joining their husbands on a trip. We always have things to do, he said to comfort me, his wife Miriam was the same way.

I asked Carlos to take me to an area of the reserve that you visited together before your fateful journey. You had told me about a landscape of extreme beauty and on that occasion I did not go because I was cutting the patterns to sew some shirts. Later I didn't go with you because I was tired from so much sewing. Although I learned this lesson late, I now know that life is in the present. We must live in the now, because later may not exist.

Carlos and I talked about you so much, as we walked through the woods, chasing your trail. I told him my great concern to know if your murderer had taken your life quickly or you had been made to suffer. That thorn will scratch my heart until the day you and I meet again.

Carlos agrees with me that getting rid of you was not an incidental act but a premeditated one instead. There are just as many who benefited from your disappearance as those who rejoiced at your death. To define who forged it and who was simply happy about the event would require a deep delve into the scale of each one's conscience, even if your death is beyond remedy.

He told me that two young volunteers had arrived from the United States. I wanted to go say hello to them and, as you can imagine, I was so moved to see them. We talked to them about the conservation of the reserve. They told me of the animals they had seen with their astonished eyes. I love talking to these young people who are so healthy, so full of life and with such a curious disposition for everything that is new and the desire to help protect wildlife. Hope is rekindled in me that these new generations know the value of life, in the same way you and I always appreciated it. When they spoke about the garrobos, they did so with the same pronunciation as yours: "gorobitos" and I didn't know whether to laugh or cry. It was very gratifying to see how beautiful everything is. I know you are watching from your hilltop.

Now I am going to tell you about something that surprised me on my return:

There is a man who works at the dock in Puntarenas hauling sacks of rice and beans that are unloaded from the boats, as well as luggage carried by travelers. Since I moved to Puntarenas, I see him frequently and we greet each other, although we have never had a conversation.

On my return from our house in Cocalito a week ago, while he was helping me off the boat with my bags, he confessed to me that he was the brother-in-law of Omar, your executioner. Lowering his voice, he told me that in July, Omar had arrived in Puntarenas a week before your death with the intention of visiting his father in Punta Llorona. On that occasion, he returned to Pavas, which was where he lived with his wife, without boarding the boat from Puntarenas to Punta Llorona and with no explanation for cancelling the trip. His sister, Omar's wife, that little girl who I saw scared and crying the day of his arrest in Pavas, had told him that the following week Omar left again. He left in a hurry to Puntarenas, without bathing or changing his clothes, to embark for Punta Llorona because his father was waiting for him. The man spoke quickly, with a low, monotone voice, as if he needed to urgently drop a load too heavy for his conscience to bear.

It is not difficult to connect the dots from this confession. Sometimes I regret not having sought to raise the money to appeal the sentence of your murderer and to search for his possible accomplices. I am sure that a good investigator would find, with the clues that I have, the real culprits: the instigators. But I was nullified for a while, with no ability to react and bristling at the smallest nocturnal noise. I couldn't even get mad at the killer, a crazy guy who didn't even know your name. I was always sure that he was only the executioner, but nobody wanted to listen. Not a single hand was outstretched to me.

Your Voyage to Punta Llorona

I can't stop thinking about the conversation I told you about, with the man who hauls sacks on the dock. I have linked what he told me to other events during that time period. I don't know if you remember, but I do. You planned to travel precisely that first week, but you postponed it because of the matter with that boy's horse, Manuel I think his name was. It was a very old horse full of bruises and when you saw him tied up in front of Camilo's grocery store, you took off his saddle and left it on the dirt floor. You were leading the horse away by the reins, when the little boy, about twelve years old, came out with his grocery bag. He yelled at you that the horse belonged to his father. You told him that neither he nor his father had the right to mistreat the horse that way, and that you would pay his father what he was worth. You left the boy crying with rage and impotence, because he had to carry the load to his house in Delicias, up in the mountains. You told me about it when you got home with that poor horse, which had bleeding ulcers on its left haunch, to whom you had been speaking to with the same affection that you used when you spoke to me. Your sympathies were not reserved for humans, with few exceptions.

It was at the dock in Puntarenas that the boy's father found you that day you were going to board the boat to Corcovado and he confronted you. He said that you had stolen something from him and that he was going to the police station to report you. You offered to pay him for the horse and after showing him your cards from various animal protection societies, little by little he calmed down and understood your compassionate feelings towards the animal. You told me that there was a certain shame in the man because of the accusation of mistreatment that you made against him, confronting him with his cruelty towards the animals that helped to make our lives easier and invested so much loyalty towards insensitive humans. I am used to hearing your speech, but he was taken aback by it. By the time the matter was cleared up and you apologized to each other, the ship to Corcovado had already sailed. There wasn't another boat leaving until the following week, so you came home.

You finally made the trip to Corcovado on July 21 and Omar got on the same boat. After your murder was made public, those who piloted the boat said he boarded when it was about to set sail. He was sitting next to you throughout the journey, watching you while you drew in your notebook and asking you for information about your life here.

Witnesses said that when you arrived at Punta Llorona you stopped at Fernando Vargas' ranch, the boy that I had met on my previous trip to Carate who knew the area very well. He had accompanied me to look for avocado seeds on the first visit, when I went alone. But his father informed you that he was away and would not be back for two days. So, Omar, who was following you vigilantly, offered to accompany you on a tour of the forest and you accepted, because you didn't want to waste time. Once you decided on a plan of action, you refused to deviate from it. For you it was strategic planning, as if you were still in the military.

I know that there are tiny and fortuitous events that change the course of history, but I doubt this was one of them. The strangest thing is that apart from Carlos, the park ranger, I am the only person who does not believe the official version of the event of your death. It is inconceivable that the National Parks administration had not demanded that the Government investigate the true causes of your death. Who knows if your murder was linked to the discontent caused by the lousy management of compensation for the expropriations? None of them have offered me any support in this misfortune.

The second wife of Omar's stepfather assured investigators in her statement that Omar had returned alone from the beach and told her you were exploring the forest. Omar had paid the woman to cook a chicken for him, but when he got back he said he had to return urgently to Pavas that same night. She had cooked the chicken but was surprised when Omar left without eating and walked all night to Drake to board the boat to Puntarenas the next day. That urgency to leave caught her attention. At least that was what she repeated, over and over again, to all who would listen. I heard her repeat that mantra, which sounded rehearsed to me, as she impatiently wrung her hands under her ashen apron. Omar wasn't her son and it showed. The corners of her lips curved while she said his name with a cold look of distance which revealed the absence of affection.

When asked about her husband Enrique, Omar's stepfather, her body betrayed her, however. Her flesh loosened and she put both hands to her chest, assuring that he was in the cabin with her and the little ones the whole time, splitting firewood for the kitchen.

I didn't like that Enrique's look, baleful and elusive. I was suspicious of the accusation he made about his stepson that he seemed to have made during a night of drinking. While we were around a campfire on the beach waiting for the boat to pick us up, to take your remains to the Forensic Institute, it was the first time I feared for my life. Being accompanied by the two investigators and by Salvador Díaz did not make me feel any safer.

Any detective who had carried out a thorough, conscientious investigation would have easily obtained the information I collected and reached the conclusion that the intellectual culprits of your infamous and absurd death are still at large. As you can see, I wasn't so far off the mark when I insisted on the investigation. I always knew there was something else that didn't come to light, even if the police treated me like an obsessive maniac. I can't tell if knowing the truth would allow me to live without the regrets and doubts of having done less than I could have. I know that if it had been the other way around, if I had been murdered, you would not leave a single stone unturned until you avenged my death. I don't have your physical or emotional strength. Everyone gives what they can and I gave you all my love, every day we shared.

Sometimes we accept reality too easily, without questioning how much truth there is in the evidence, which is not always what it appears to be. But it is useless for you and I to delve deeper into history. I'm going to sleep. Tomorrow is Thursday and Pablo, Nery's son, will bring me the mail along with the cheese and tortillas that my good friend affectionately prepares for me.

Cabinas Karen

1979

*M*y dear love, yesterday I learned from Pablo, Nery's boy, that some people have entered our farm and occupied our house. Although our neighbors got them to vacate, I don't know if they will be able to keep the squatters away. Squatting is backed by the law, as you know, and it is a customary practice in this country. If a piece of land is abandoned, it is at risk of being occupied and over time it becomes the property of the occupiers. I have been dreading this moment ever since I moved to Puntarenas, but I wanted to believe that it would not happen. Now I know that I must do something to avoid it before it happens again.

I am considering returning to our house in Cocalito, but I have yet to find an activity that allows me to earn a living. I doubt that I can find students for my English and yoga classes there, and it is even less likely that they can pay me.

I have some savings, but they won't go far. I must come up with a way to make money, I'm sure the idea will come at the right time. I'll throw out a net tonight into the sea of my dreams, to see if I catch an idea that will help me return. Meanwhile, I will notify the landlords and my students since they will need time to look for another school. As I prepare to leave, I am grateful because thanks to them I have been able to start my life again.

I am packing what little I have here in Puntarenas, next week I leave for Cocalito. I am excited and a little worried about the uncertainty in the life that awaits me. But I think that precisely this uncertainty will mark the rest of my life, and I accept it, knowing that life can be restarted again and again. People who always know where they are going never discover anything. The obstacles we find in the middle of the road are placed there to be overcome and that is precisely the adventure of life.

I leaf through letters and photos in the folder again, arranged chronologically, as if they were relatives who move with me wherever I go. They are my only valuable possessions.

There is a photo in which I smile at the camera and you are hugging me, while looking at me with the love that radiated from your eyes when they rested on me. No one but you has ever looked at me with such veneration, as if your eyes projected a protective beacon to keep me from evil. I can't remember who the photographer was. Maybe Frank?

There is also one where I am tending the honey production. I look so young and excited; I have the smile of a happy girl. We shared the honey with the workers, because as we gradually increased the hives and there was enough for everyone. In those days, the workers produced much of their own food which covered most of the basic needs for their homes, but they did not have honey.

They had not yet invented the necessities that came later. The television and its harmful influence had not yet arrived to alert them of all their shortcomings. What a great opportunity it would have been to use the television to educate people! They watched it mesmerized, procuring an altar for it in the premier location of their homes.

Oh, my love, I live a double life in my dreams… they are so real, so vivid, I feel as if I lived twice, once during the day and once at night. I really believe that there is no difference between what has been lived and what has been dreamed. Because life could be a dream…or a nightmare; and dreams come true as if they were prophecies. As I write, my small bit of luggage is already at the door and I am about to depart. I must write, because last night my dream surprised me and I'm afraid I will forget it with all the hustle and bustle.

I was in a white house, but it was not our cabin, it was bigger. It was a house with many doors and a group of people lined up to enter along the corridor and the garden, which was full of bushes and almond trees. Once inside, they settled into their rooms. Although there were many people, dressed in colorful tribal clothes from different continents, there was space for everyone and I handed them sheets and indigo blue towels, saying "Welcome to my house".

I awoke amazed at the lucidity of my dream and convinced that this is what I must do. Open a simple guest house for people who cannot afford the hotel, which is most of those who arrive in

Montezuma. I have to make a list of things I will need to buy in San José: sheets, towels and curtains for the windows, but first I have to find an inexpensive house to rent in the center of Montezuma.

My love, I was right about my dream and everything is coming together. I went to visit Frank and Tina when I returned to Montezuma, as they are some of the best friends we have here. I noticed that they recently built a little house in the center of Montezuma, which is perfect for me. It's small, white, and I proposed to trade the house for our upper lot, the corner one, which is bigger. They accepted because they are eager for me to come back and live near them. They say that we showed them how to live and to value what they have and they are very grateful to us. Before our arrival, they traded their land for old cars and useless junk which might work for a month and then they had nothing. I found their words so moving that I couldn't hold back the tears from rolling down my face and they wept too. All three of us knew that the tears were for you, because you couldn't be there to hear such beautiful words.

There are no walls yet inside the house, so I'll have to do something to divide it into rooms. I'll also have to find the money to equip it. Today I have an insurmountable wall before me, and I can't find the solution. I trust that my dreams will help me find the key. It wouldn't be the first time, right? Good night my love.

Oh Olof, I don't know if you will believe it, I can hardly believe it myself. Among the correspondence that Camilo had saved for me in Montezuma, there was a huge, wonderful surprise: a letter that arrived two weeks ago from the Swedish National Pensions Office, the *Pensionsmyndigheten*. After all the usual greetings, they ask me for the bank details to transfer my widow's pension for your death, retroactive for more than three years. They also apologize for not being able to reach me earlier.

I know that our friends from the Speleby group have done all the paperwork and have not given up despite the tedious boredom of dealing with bureaucracy. I feel indebted to them, although I know they do it because of their true friendship and in honor of your memory. It is not a large pension, but since it is retroactive, I have enough to equip the guest house. I will tell you confidentially: I believe that the Universe is on my side; it spins in my favor and things are falling into place to make my life easier. This must be an attempt to compensate, since my biggest treasure was taken.

I must tell you something that happened which has overtaken my thoughts for several days. I am obsessed again. I went to San José with Tina to sign the acceptance of the bank transfer from the *Pensionsmyndigheten* and to buy what I need to equip the rooms. We were buying fruit at the Mercado del Mayoreo, on Avenida 12, near the Cementerio Obrero, and I ran into the man who hauled the sacks from the boat to the warehouse in Puntarenas. Yes, the brother-in-law of Omar, your killer. He was still pushing his cart, carrying fruits and vegetables from one place to another, as if it were his only possible destiny in life. This country is so small that we all meet up, wherever we go.

It was a rainy day, and despite the umbrella and the confusion from the rain, he recognized me instantly. He told me, under the torn burlap sack that covered his head and part of his back, that his brother-in-law had been killed in prison, in a fight with another inmate in which they both died. He spoke like before, stealthily, lowering his voice, in a steady stream, without stopping, as if he had released a burden. It must be his manner of speaking.

A little over three years have passed since the sentence and you see, he didn't even complete it. In the end, it would have been absurd to appeal for a longer sentence to be imposed. What would have been the point? There are wise decisions that life makes on our behalf, even if we believe the decisions are ours.

It would have been another thing unmask those who are hiding in the shadows. His sudden death seems more like a reckoning between criminals or perhaps a way to silence him forever. Codes of silence have a shelf life and the truth is unveiled when it expires. I wouldn't be surprised if those who paid to kill you sent another assassin to guarantee eternal silence. What surprises me even more is that nothing appeared in the newspapers, despite the coverage your murder received. You were the first conservationist to be sacrificed in this country. If your death was widely publicized, it is strange that his death was not. Possibly someone has taken it upon themselves to bury it, in every sense of the word. But if they can keep the news from getting out, that makes me think that someone very powerful was involved in your murder.

I don't know if it's true or not. Truth doesn't matter anymore because no truth, hidden or announced, will bring you back to me. I tried to talk to him in prison, after he was sentenced, when I accompanied a Swedish journalist as a translator during an interview. I tried hard; I couldn't just let things be. Although I insisted, he said that he had nothing to say to me and did not receive me. He said he was paying for his crime, and I should leave him in peace. How impudent, to mention peace and the right to life when he took both things from us. I will go to my grave believing that someone was very interested in making you disappear you from this world and now the time came for your executioner, although not for the one who decided your murder.

Today I know that happiness is a fleeting state that leaves the heart afflicted and empty when it passes. That is why it is important to learn to accept. Confucius said that only he who can be happy with everything can always be happy, so acceptance is the key to existence. If I must be honest, my current state is very similar to happiness or serenity.

Tourists arrive in waves looking for a cheaper place to stay than the hotel, so I take them in and explain the house rules. They can use the kitchen, the plates, and cups, but they must leave everything as tidy as they find it. They also have to respect my cats, which grow and multiply at the same rate as humans do. I have to do something about it. I imagine that spaying the cats will be the easiest solution, even if it pains me to do so.

I have a Nicaraguan maid who helps me clean the rooms and the kitchen three hours a day. Her name is Reina and she has three children with three short years separating the oldest from the youngest, who is one year old. Each one has a different father, but they are all hers; a situation so common that it is not strange to me anymore. She is a determined woman who looks me in the eye; the fact that she is my employee does not make her feel inferior in any way. I like her sincere and worthy gaze. Each of us does our own thing and we both feel rewarded.

Sometimes, some of the younger tourists accompany me to Cocalito and enjoy spending time with *Lis*. But the moment they are not looking she opens the zippers of their bags. When she finds what she wants, she grabs it and climbs the nearest tree, so they can't get to her. Sometimes it is cigarettes and I worry that she's going to eat them, or that she's going to bite into something that might hurt her. But I have a strategy that never fails to get her down. I pretend I'm crying and then she quickly comes to my side. She can't bear to see me cry.

One day a visitor's gold pen disappeared and he couldn't find it anywhere. It was a memory of his youth, with great sentimental and monetary value. We searched for the pen for a long time, unable to find it. Then I told him about *Lis'* habits. He looked at me incredulously and probably thought I was crazy. I ignored his gesture and pretended to cry. Sitting in the hallway, I covered my face with my hands and began to moan as I leaned on the table. To my delight, and to demonstrate to the man the absurdity of his mistrust, two minutes later *Lis* was handing me the pen. He couldn't believe it, even as he saw it. Sometimes reality is difficult to accept.

This week we had more tourists than ever and I rented out my room in Montezuma and our guest house in Cocalito. I came to Cocalito with a couple. They are very young and seem very respectful. When they saw *Lis* arrive at the house they were excited and didn't quite know how to behave. *Lis*, on the other hand, behaves perfectly naturally and always knows her place.

If I can choose who to host, I prefer couples to single girls or boys. If they are single, visitors of the opposite sex are continuously coming in and out of the house. In the end I don't even know which ones are guests and which are sporadic visitors, because they all look alike. The situation bothers me and I will have to change the rules for visitors in the cabins, so it does not become unpleasant for me... Oh, what a ridiculous claim; as if this were a Hilton chain hotel. But I will do it, for the sake of maintaining a certain order and respect in my house, because after all it is my house. I don't want to dictate the rules of convenience for their lives, of course. Because I know that he who lives doing only what is convenient has a miserable life. But everything has a balance point and my rights end where the neighbor's rights begin. I suppose I have become very philosophical.

What surprises me more every day is to see how young people visit here from distant lands such as Israel or Turkey. Of course, Denmark is not exactly next door either.

A Dutch Woman in Montezuma

1980

A Dutch girl arrived in Montezuma. Her name is Patricia and she works at the Hotel Las Lapas, on the road to Cabuya. She is cute, cheerful, and very young. She came over smiling to talk to me, even though I didn't feel like talking to her or anyone. I was sad that day because one of my cats, who was very old, had passed away. She didn't know of my sad disposition, and as the conversation progressed she told me that she had studied nutrition at The House of Raw Food, in Humlegården. Can you imagine such a coincidence? How is it possible that the three of us have been to this unique place in the world? The intentions of this universal cosmic order, whose laws govern our lives without our consent, are not easily understood. If we had planned to meet, surely it would have been impossible. The fact that she was in the place where you and I fell in love makes me like her already. Finally, I have someone nearby with whom I can talk about that paradoxical place without having to explain all the details of that lifestyle, and without receiving blank stares, as if I were an alien. Because only those who have been there can understand its eccentric objectives of achieving a long, healthy life.

We share anecdotes that we experienced in different eras, of course. We laughed to tears when I told her how I discovered several trays with cakes and sweets, which were strictly prohibited in that diet regiment, under the bed of a patient admitted to the clinic. The treatment completely excluded any food besides raw fruits and vegetables, as decreed by the clinic management in the daily menus.

We also laughed at the thick smell of garlic in the air. Everyone there ate between one and two heads of raw garlic per day, and the smell would cling to the sheets and walls. It was terrible when a new client arrived. They always had trouble breathing and spent the first few days with their nose pinched, until they got used to it, like everyone else.

We recalled Dr. Nolfi's performance when she delivered her speech at the dining room with that tiple voice: "the best food is completely natural, unprocessed. It is easier to digest. It cooperates in the expulsion of waste, as a baby cooperates in childbirth...". The comparison of the expulsion of feces with the birth of a baby seemed like tremendous nonsense and it kept us laughing for a good while. I don't understand how the people in the dining room could keep their composure without bursting out in laughter right in her face.

Patricia told me that things had changed quite a bit when she was there, fifteen years after we were. Some rules imposed by the director, the strict and eccentric Dr. Kristine Nolfi, had to be relaxed. From what I learned, there were problems with some patients who did not withstand the treatment. One patient died and his relatives filed lawsuits against the clinic, which defended itself alleging that the patient arrived in a very deteriorated state and could not recover. The truth is that I am no longer interested in anything that happens in Europe, it has nothing to do with me.

After meeting Patricia, I returned home relaxed and light, as if the weight of life had lessened. There's nothing like a hearty dose of laughter that shakes your whole body, releasing endorphins. I have also realized that her joy is contagious, and it lingered in the air a few moments before we said goodbye, the same way a halo lingers after a lightbulb is turned off.

Olof, I write in this diary and I can't tell if these words are destined for you or for me. I write as if my life depended on it. I write hoping to condense the events I experience, infusing them with a dramatic force that perhaps they never had. I still stretch my arm to find you when I awake in the morning, although you have been gone for six years now. Every morning I feel a pinch of anguish that makes me nauseous. As strange as it may seem, I know that years later our memories will not represent events as we lived them, but as they are depicted in these writings. Our brain toys with us and we can do nothing to avoid it. On many mornings before your fateful trip, you were already gone when I awoke, yet I didn't feel that pinch of sadness in the pit of my stomach because I knew you would return.

The worst is giving up hope, knowing that there will never be another time and my fingers won't feel the wrinkles on your skin again. That's why I hold on to rancor for your killers, even if I can't put faces or names on them. They only knew part of what you were and will have likely forgotten you already. My memory, however, reminds me of my loss heedlessly every morning. Why do we always live outside of the present? What perverse mechanism do we harbor within ourselves that makes us relive the past or think about the future, while we wait for life to evolve in the one direction or another? He who takes the life of another does not consider that their life or its absence transcends beyond their victim. Taking a life also ends that which lived because of his presence, the brightness spread by his own vital halo. Just as when a spell is cast, it is not the words that heal but the energy they dispel.

Perhaps that's why my mood swings aimlessly, like a weathervane shaken by the wind. One day I feel a singing joy that overflows me, the next day, I sink into apathy and silence. I crash into the extremes while searching for balance.

"No life so boring that it cannot be transformed into art by a lively imagination" my mother used to say when as a child I complained about the monotony of life. But at some stages art is not enough to illuminate all the silences. Only a fortunate few are chosen by the muses.

Yesterday, I awoke shaken by the affliction of your absence. It was like a magma of sadness rising from my sandals, sticking to my ankles, and traveling the entire length of my skin. I couldn't shake it off, although I tried throughout the morning. In a fit of nostalgia and in a jumble of emotions, I decided to look for the box with our photographs. I felt so bad already that it couldn't possibly get any worse.

I wrote the names of the places on the back of some of them, so as not to forget. I see you in California in December 1954 and my heart melts with love, like a piece of ice in the sun. You're bare-chested and your muscular arms lift me up into the air. You walked me around the garden, ignoring my protests. I felt that if heaven existed, then you embodied it. You have lifted me up with your words and with your arms, but now what? What does life expect me to do? What is the script that it has written for me?

Dusk is falling and the bright light fades to amber. I feel a languor of drowsy silence in the same place where mad ideas previously fluttered, like birds in disarray, crashing into each other on a flight to nowhere. Yes, if I must choose, I prefer this laxity that loosens all my joints. Sometimes it is good to stop and recover strength. This hour of rest was my favorite hour when you were by my side because it was when we dedicated the rest of the day to each other.

I unfold a letter from your father dated March 12, 1972:

Dear Olle and Karen, thank you for making me aware about the situation with the inheritance of Waldemar, Karen's father, in your letter from February 29. We all knew that no one in the family liked that Karen emigrated to Costa Rica, but it is unfair that they do not want to distribute the inheritance as it should correspond by right and will...

I stopped reading to avoid mortifying myself with the fight between my brothers over my father's inheritance. The widow who did everything possible so that I did not receive an equal part, was worst of all. But she didn't succeed, as I am reminded by the response you wrote your father. I should have read the reply first.

There are more loving letters exchanged with your father, attached to your responses, from January to April. Fortunately, you always kept the draft, so I can have them all. In the last one you write:

We are still sleeping outside, in the forest, with the owls, bats, skunks, coyotes and pumas. On April 13, with the new moon, the first rains will arrive and our friends from the forest will no longer have our company, until next dry season...

Yes, back then the rains came when they were expected, and one could foresee the best time to plant. But little by little everything is changing, especially the climate, and this change will be decisive in the life of all inhabitants of this planet. If the life model of human beings does not change, I am afraid that life in this planet will be annihilated. The push for consumerism as the possible route to happiness will lead to the collapse of the planet. I hope I'm not here for that.

I find a letter in my handwriting dated April 10, 1972, in which I congratulate your father on his eighty-fifth birthday. I explain in detail what a bouquet of flowers look like here, with vibrant colors and leaves in different shades of green. Olive, citrine greens, intense silver, and golden. Others are simply green, such as the leaves of lemon trees or those of star apples, green on the upper side, dark and earthy on the underside, or bright emerald green... Because I couldn't send him the bouquet, I drew it on the paper with my words...

...the reddest hibiscus and the defiant heliconias, which stretch out their beaks, like floral parrots; the tiny orchids with exquisite filigree that are born in the trees and adorn them to take part in the dance of life. The profusion of Impatiens flowers line the paths, embroidering them in every possible shade of pink, from pale to fuchsia and different shades of red...

Before I realize it, I have tears running streaming down from my eyes to my chin, neck, and chest. I know that I must not continue down this road, wallowing in pain and flooded with tears.

I force myself to go for a walk, before the sun disappears between the sea line and the horizon, like a splendid gold coin in a giant money box. That line of the horizon, keeper of our time lived and of our hopes; some fulfilled, others discarded.

I return calmed by the rhythm of the waves. The dragging of tiny particles of shells that make up the sand, caressing the beach with the leisurely rhythm of a waltz, neither slow nor fast, that cadence of sustained movement...

Once again, today I relied on nature to calm the agony of my spirit. I feel ridiculous for my complaints about life when I see the beautiful and fragile butterflies, so dignified in their way of being, and the industrious leaf-cutter ants carrying bits of leaves several times their own size. If they can take charge of their lives, shouldn't I be able to do it too?

I have seen Patricia with Lenny, that American musician that arrived a couple of years ago. They make a cute couple and look at each other like you and I did, as if the rest of the world were transparent or simply did not exist. They only have eyes for each other. They are selling fruit for a living, and it seems that they are doing well. Every day I see many customers at their stand. I hope they stay because I feel I can relate to them in some respects.

You and I decided to live here, but there are aspects of our European culture that are not understood by the locals. It is only logical, because the culture and education learned from the first years of life to adolescence are essential in shaping opinions, beliefs, and lifestyles. The European lifestyle no longer identifies me, however, this is my chosen lifestyle, which has nothing to do with my Danish origin. In Montezuma the contours are blurred, just as Patricia and Lenny's lifestyle are not predetermined by their origin. I enjoy my conversations with them, which have become part of our routine, and I wait for them in the evenings so we can share what the day has brought us.

Whenever they leave town for work or errands, I miss them and look forward to their return. They are the closest thing to distant relatives. They are closer to me emotionally than my biological family, as you know. They say you cannot choose your family, but you can choose your friends. Unwanted friends are not forced on us, but family remains until the last day of each of its members. I was very happy because they bought a lot in Playa Colorada, next to us, and they are going to build a house. I hope they buy the lot for sale next to my cabins, that way we would always be near each other.

Olof, you will not believe what happened this week. On Tuesday I was in our forest, near the creek, collecting pochote buds for vegetable smoothies. I went very early in the morning; the sun had barely risen. I had already filled my bag and was about to head home. Suddenly, I heard the neigh of a horse; very close by, about a hundred meters. I approached stealthily and there it was indeed. A brown horse, not very old, with a saddle and a white star on its forehead. It was tied to a young jiñocuabe tree with an old and dirty cord. It reminded me of Lucero, that gentle horse that we bought from Camilo shortly after arriving here. I imagined it belonged to a hunter and I decided to get some help, so I wouldn't be alone if he confronted me. After your murder I have learned to be prudent.

I fetched Patricia, told her my plan and we returned together. We untied the horse and lead it by the reins to the patio of the house. More than two hours passed, and the sun was already high when the owner came looking for the horse. We were sitting in the corridor waiting for him. He didn't have anything in his hands, but he took off his hat when he greeted us with a "Buenas." He approached determined and said that that was his horse, but we didn't let him say anything else. We jumped on his possible arguments, cornering him and telling him that he had entered private property, which was a crime punishable by prison. We informed him that if we found him trespassing again, nothing and no one would save him from going to jail. We were like two machine guns. When one of us spoke, the other was silent. But we gave him no respite.

He apologized, his voice as thin as a thread. He untied the horse slowly and led him away with his back hunched and his feet shuffling, as if his old black boots weighed two tons. He couldn't have been twenty years old, skinny and with a clipped mustache that split his sunburned face in two. He got on the horse and when we could hardly see him anymore or hear the horse trotting, Patricia and I looked at each other. We reflected on the fact that he was not a bad person, as he could have easily depleted us, but he respected our arguments. The truth is, I never saw him on our property again.

I found out later he was saying that I was "crazy." Yes, a dangerous madwoman, surely…ha, ha. He is not the only one who thinks so. Since I returned from Puntarenas I have heard that nickname on more than one occasion.

I have quite the story for you today. Two days ago, they organized a cockfight in Montezuma, another cursed tradition from the Spanish conquerors. I was tired of hearing the shouts of the men exhorting the roosters, a reddish one and a black one, so I went out there and found an arena made of stones and straw near the beach. A bunch of men with distorted faces surrounded the arena, yelling and howling like coyotes. Worst of all, children of all ages also witnessed the terrifying spectacle. I saw a black-feathered rooster lying in a puddle of his own blood and the other, a reddish one, stalking him. A shouting argument ensued between the owners of the roosters, so I took advantage of the moment and entered the arena. I grabbed the red rooster by the legs and carried it home with me under my arm. When the owner noticed it was gone, he ran around aimlessly until someone finally directed him to me. He arrived panting and sweaty, clutching a hand full of old, crumpled bills in one hand. With the other hand he tried to snatch the rooster from me, as I was about to enter the house. I threw the rooster inside and turned on him, telling him that I was going to report him to the police and to stay away from me or I would shoot him.

They all know that cockfighting is prohibited by law. Not so much because of the damage and brutality to the animals, but because of the consequences on families. Men tend to gamble, spend their weekly pay and leave their families penniless, without enough to buy rice for their children. Gambling drives them crazy, and I have even heard that many even lose their jobs because of this disastrous vice.

He muttered: "The crazy one. I had heard there was a crazy person here." He must have truly believed that I would shoot him. That's how I found out the name that those who mistreat animals have given me. I accept it, with all the consequences it carries.

A few days later the rooster disappeared. I think maybe he rescued him from the yard, where I had left him to roam free, as it should be. My only hope is that the owner doesn't come back here with the same intentions.

Karen and Patricia at a children's theater presentation.

A baby in the family

1982

*T*oday is July 23, the seventh anniversary of your death, Olof. Time moves continuously, but it is deceptive, because it seems like it stands still. I recognize that over the years this is a day like any other. Another day you are not with me, living only in my memory. Every single thing I do each day I do on behalf of both of us. Although I am sure you would not approve of all my actions, I have to take some license in my own name.

Also, a year ago today, a news story appeared in La Nación reporting that Corcovado National Park had been invaded by squatters again, in search of gold which they believe to be hidden under the cover of the forest. They discussed in detail the methods used to extract the gold. One method is by using extremely powerful pumps to inject enormous amounts of pressurized water, causing erosion that washes trees and soil into the rivers... I put the newspaper aside and stopped reading, so as not to rekindle my theory about your death and those who caused it.

But yesterday, a tourist brought some bananas wrapped in pages from last Sunday's newspaper and they talked about the same thing again. Perhaps they just rehash the story once a year, when they have nothing else to talk about. The article dealt with the origins of gold panning in this country's rivers, specifically in Corcovado's Tigre River. Entomologist Álvaro Wille Trejos tells the story that begins in 1937. It was then that the word got out attracting more than four hundred gold miners from Nicaragua and Panama. I remember the number circulating after your death was around sixty miners. This article that I am reading today does not speak of a specific figure currently, but the report assures that the "coligalleros" as they are called, have operated clandestinely in small groups and that larger waves have arrived occasionally. He also assures that they have advanced towards Río Claro, whose course is suffering the same disastrous consequences. I pity this beautiful river, so full of life, whose image I cherish in my retina. Even if my visit was linked to a fateful situation: trying and failing to unravel the circumstances surrounding your death.

I was blocked for a few moments after I read the article. This scientist's brave indictment about the peril of Corcovado's rainforests puts him in a situation of risk that he may not even imagine. I don't know if he is aware of the danger that may be stalking him, but I have shuddered while reading it, from my feet to the last hair on my head. People have a short memory, especially if something does not directly affect them. Here, people who make too much noise are killed just like that, without giving it much thought. The investigator then archives the file and moves on to the next case. Deaths and sins occur every day and the next generation buries the previous one.

I am convinced this is the reason the protection of the reserves is not taken seriously because they are managed by Executive Decree but the decree is not protected by law. In the case of Corcovado, the reserve was created on October 24, 1975, by order of decree 5357A. They are not taken seriously by the squatters, nor the gold miners in Corcovado, not even the Administration itself. Because decrees are not endowed with a budget or with the necessary resources to fight criminals. Confronting outlaws who carry firearms and will not hesitate to use them to achieve their goals is not a task that a few park rangers can handle, not even with their best intentions and vigilance. This is a task for the leaders of this country.

Finally, they created the Institute of Lands and Colonization, which precisely this year, has been renamed the Institute of Agrarian Development. I believe that this definition is more contemporary and consistent with the performance of the institution.

Alas, we have done our part for Corcovado. Much more than I, at least, would have wanted. The price of your life was excessive. They named Corcovado a reserve two months after your murder, perhaps driven by the shame of the event and its international repercussions. They never offered me their support to investigate the details of your death. They said that the culprit was already in prison "what more does that woman want, if the killer himself detailed how he killed him? Nobody is stupid enough or crazy enough to take the blame if they are innocent…" I have heard this repeatedly.

On the other hand, their attitude towards the conservation of the forests makes me believe that they are making miniscule steps, attempting to cover the entire distance of the earth from one end to the other. When you get halfway through the journey the other half no longer exists.

It is not that different from what is happening to us in Cabo Blanco. We are just as unprotected, but luckily here the situation is easier to control. It is not that we have more resources, but Corcovado's 42,000-hectare area is not comparable and complicates things. The years and the effort we have invested in defending Cabo Blanco also marks a difference between the two reserves.

Olof, a month ago I told you that we needed a law to stop the gold miners and today I found out that it was approved two weeks ago. This is great news for all of us because it is the law of the land which affects every reserve and monument. I must rectify what I said about our leaders, but only on this occasion and without setting a precedent…ha, ha.

I don't know if I had mentioned, Olof, but Frank has been collecting newspaper articles related to Corcovado for some time. He brings them over because he thinks they might be of interest to me, and they are. The one he brought me today is great news. They have published the book *Corcovado: Meditations of a Biologist*, by Álvaro Wille Trejos. He is the entomologist I told you about some time ago who denounced the gold miners. Today the information is out in the press. I hope that this publication does not put his life at risk. I can't wait to lay eyes on the book. When I go to San José I will stop by Lehmann to buy it; I hope it's not too expensive. I am very curious to read what he has to say about Corcovado. If you want to know the truth, I consider the progress in that reserve an advance payment of the debt the reserve contracted with you.

Apparently, Wille's relationship with the University of Kansas began when a professor from that school arrived in Puerto Limón on a collecting expedition with a group of researchers carrying out an investigation on the tropical rain forest. He was just a boy who was hired to help them in the search for different species. He later went on to study at the University of Kansas, where he earned a masters and doctorate in entomology. He worked with a research team in Mesoamerica to unravel the evolution of social life in insects. He had extensive experience in the field because he had been observing insects in the forests and pastures since he was a child. It so important for young people to be passionate about their environment! It is essential, so that they may concentrate their efforts to the protection of the life that surrounds them. It is also essential that patrons or tutors accompany them on the path of their training. In the long run, this is beneficial for everyone, because a well-trained group of young people has many possibilities to improve their culture, economic status, as well as the economy of the country as a whole. The former president José María Figueres Ferrer coined that legendary phrase long before we got here: "What is the use of tractors if there are no violins?" It is paradoxical, as he was an agriculturist, but I fear that his vision no longer bears the impact it once did.

Patricia has brought me wonderful news today, Olof, she is going to have a baby. While it is true that there is no shortage of babies and children of all ages in this town, there will finally be one close to my life. I feel like I'm going to be a grandmother because little by little, with our daily coexistence, they have become my family. Since they bought the land next door, we have shared so much time together. We confide in each other about events from our past as well as everyday occurrences. As you know, women need friends to share with.

I was telling her a few days ago about our amazement when we just arrived and got to know our neighbors and their families. They all had a minimum of eight children. Women became mothers as little girls; some had their first child at fourteen. We checked our closest neighbors and realized that just four women had birthed fifty-eight living children: Dulcelina, twelve children; Claudia, thirteen; Elisa, twelve; Leonella, twenty-one. The population density in this country must be the highest in the world.

This is, however, a beautiful place to raise a child, with so much life pulsing everywhere. Everything is so close that mothers don't need to leave their children in a nursery to work. In fact, in many cases working moms take their kids with them. Something has changed, thankfully. Before, those with few children were looked down upon. They reproached them, calling them "tramps", as if they had not fulfilled their duty as expected.

Olof, I am hopeful that, albeit slowly, a new consciousness is awakening in people. This year two books on conservation were published in close succession. Both are extraordinary for their content and the credibility of the authors. I have already told you about the first one, at least about the author, Álvaro Wille, because I have not yet had a chance to go to San José to look for the book. But I just found out that Daniel Janzen, along with a consortium of researchers, has published *The Natural History of Costa Rica*. This publication makes me think of the primary and secondary schools in this country. At some point students will have the opportunity to read and appreciate their natural heritage. Because they will only take care of their environment if they cultivate a sense of belonging to that which surrounds them. Unfortunately, that which belongs to everyone is left with no one to defend it, except in the indigenous peoples. It is a long-term job, but the returns are guaranteed.

Janzen's book is in English, but I hope that one day it will be published in Spanish. English is not a language spoken by the common people. If we want to save wildlife every social class must cooperate, but especially the most humble, those who live in contact with nature and who will feel the consequences of its loss more virulently.

Olof, I just returned from Heredia where I met Moraya, Patricia's newborn baby boy. I was filled with emotion as I held him in my arms, as if he were my own grandson. Of course, I don't know exactly what mothers feel, since I haven't had children. I sense that it must be something close to the tenderness that flooded me when *Lis* gave birth to her kits. Moraya was born three days ago in Santa Bárbara de Heredia and I couldn't wait any longer to meet him. I hope that in a few days they will be back in Montezuma so I can spoil him; "chinearlo" as they say around here.

It is the 4th of November and the Nicaraguans who live here are celebrating the victory of the Sandinista Party in that country's first free elections. Daniel Ortega will be the president starting in January of next year. Hopefully those suffering people will finally have peace and prosperity. Today they are partying, tomorrow none of the men will show up at work. Reina will arrive like every other day, holding her little ones with one hand and her little parasol with the other, like the rest of the women. For them it is just another day, because no matter who wins the elections, they know their children must be fed. That's the way things are here, and no politician will change them.

1985

A new year arrived bringing with it more and more tourists. Montezuma is no longer a ghost town after the exodus of the agricultural workers, quite the opposite. There are days that we wish things were calmer, but balance is the most difficult thing to achieve. Whenever I can, I escape to Cocalito. There I can play the music of Mahler or Tchaikovsky and dance between our two houses, under the trees, and perform my energetic dance in nature to the point of exhaustion. I end up hugging the trees, energizing my spirit, so I can deal with the tourists again and attend to my cats. I have lost track of how many there are now, I think around twenty. Somedays a cat who is not part of my protégés shows up at lunchtime, but I cannot reject it, because it is a living creature, just like the rest.

I take *Mis-Mis* with me on some of my trips to Cocalito. I know you wouldn't approve, but she behaves wonderfully. She doesn't chase the squirrels or the coatis, because she has been used to *Lis* since she was born. When I speak to her, she looks at me and I am convinced that she understands me. Perhaps not word for word, she understands the substance, which is what's important. She understands me better than many people here, which is not that difficult to believe after all.

We are in May, but we are getting less rain than we need. Álvaro, the director of National Parks, agrees with me. He came to visit me last weekend with a friend from San José and her three beautiful children. Two girls and one boy. I brought them to Cocalito and set them up in the guest house. Álvaro and I went to the hill to pick some fruit for dinner, while we chatted about the situation in the Parks. He gave me some bad news about Corcovado. It appears the gold miners are still there, as many as three thousand.

As director of the National Parks, he asked Daniel Janzen for a study in order to justify a serious request for eviction, because it appears that the fauna is disappearing and the rivers are lifeless and full of sediment. The situation is very worrying and the resources available from the Government to eradicate this destructive scourge are limited.

We walked home slowly, draped in the perfume emitted by the mangoes that we carried in a basket. We could hear the shouts of happiness from the three children in the distance and their mother's voice telling them to be careful not to slip and fall. I couldn't imagine where they could slip, since they weren't playing on the rocks at the beach.

When we got home I was furious. The kids were bathing in the water fountain we have outside the guest house, the one meant for the animals to drink. A mountain of foam rose from the water and the children splashed around in it. I couldn't help myself and told them to get out of there immediately. They should have at least waited for us to arrive and ask permission, although the answer of course would have been NO!

Álvaro held back his laughter as best he could and the mother rushed to the children, ages three to eight, out of the water. When we all calmed down, they came to apologize saying that city life had desensitized their respect for wildlife. They perfectly understood my anger and apologized for the misdeed. They carefully washed the basin and refilled it with clean water. When people from the city come to the forest, it's a headache. As the saying goes here, "it's like herding pigs."

Joaquín Alvarado

*M*y love, today I have good news: the National Parks finally sent an administrator for the reserve. Carlos introduced him to me. He a young man, about thirty years old, and his name is Joaquín. He has indigenous features, with long black hair parted in the middle and held back with a ribbon on his forehead. He wears several necklaces around his neck with amulets made of teeth and fangs that I could not identify. I like his voice, clean, warm, soft, and slow. His wide, white-toothed smile peeks out easily through his thick, curly beard and lights up the world. He has a tender, benevolent and wise look, especially striking for such a young person. His appearance is that of a man of peace, but under that black and curly hair he emanates an incorruptible will and boundless courage to defend all the creatures of the reserve.

I feel the energy that radiates from him flowing towards me like a continuous current of life. He is like a fortress, a safe place to take refuge. You would like him if you knew him; I'm sure. I think we are fortunate. He comes here after working in Poás and Corcovado. Perhaps it's a coincidence, but it is almost like he followed your trail all the way here.

His labor with the National Parks began in Santa Rosa, with Álvaro as the administrator. He volunteered there since he was fifteen years of age. Later, he worked as a farmhand. He told me that he would accept any job as long as it was outdoors and in 1978 he was appointed park ranger. By the time of his appointment, he had more knowledge than anyone else about wildlife. I think that Álvaro has the same sensitivity for the Reserve as we do, as if the reserve were his shared daughter. Surely that's why he sends us Joaquín. Today I feel lucky, I remember the fortune teller's words once again: " if your eyes and ears are open the world will reward you" and I think the gift is Joaquín.

December is here once again. I read the last thing I wrote to you just a month ago, but today I am far from that mood. Today is one of those dark and stormy days when I think I'm going to explode into a thousand pieces. It's one of those days when news of hunters in the Reserve makes me lose what little faith I have left in humanity. I know that since he arrived Joaquín does more than he can. He also tries to make me suffer as little as possible, but when it's not the hunters, it's the fishermen who wipe out every species and of all sizes by trawling. How is it possible they can't understand that they must allow the species reach adulthood, or soon will they have nothing to fish? They are doing to the sea what they previously did to the land. In a few years life will not be possible.

Many agricultural workers stopped working the land. They became fishermen and now they believe that the sea is endless, since you can't see the bottom, as is the abundance of fish. Also with tourism, people of all types and conditions have arrived.

There is a type of tourist who comes to engage in nonsense that they dare not do in their place of origin or that the laws in their countries do not allow. When these two types of people associate, with different interests but coinciding in the search of loot, any barbaric aggression against the ecosystem can occur.

Yesterday it was the queen conch that paid the consequences. They have overharvested this species in San Miguel lagoon and all over the area. They know that the queen conch is a slow-growing species which takes years to reach maturity, but they do not take any of this into consideration, because they are predatory and have no conscious. I can't tell if they don't know or don't want to know that the survival of the species is at risk if their practices continue.

Naively, I asked who might be capable of committing these atrocities and Joaquín's response was immediate: almost all of our neighbors. Sometimes I feel ashamed to belong to this group of inhabitants that are devastating this planet.

When I went to visit him yesterday, Joaquín was shooting into the air and it scared me. He told me that it was because of a boat that was fishing in the reserve. It is impossible to protect it without any resources. What is the use of declaring it a Protected Maritime Zone if there are no means to ensure that it is protected? Things remain the same, with no resources whatsoever since 1982 when the Protected Maritime Zone was declared protecting all organisms inhabiting the waters one kilometer from low tide into the sea. Joaquín arrived merely a month ago and they have already sent him veiled threats, leaving him anonymous messages written on a piece of paper and nailed to the entrance of the reserve.

Now the Government says that we have to open up the Reserve to tourism in order to generate revenue. I cannot bear the thought that after all our effort Cabo Blanco will become a tourist destination.

For better or for worse, the year is over. Let's see what the next one brings.

1986

Despite what I wrote in some euphoric moment last year, I have reached the conclusion that it was not a good year for conservation in this country. I discussed it with John and he agrees. Álvaro is on the verge of disenchantment due to the difficulties of managing the National Parks. He is battling on many fronts and in many reserves, but I know that Corcovado is a painful wound for him. In recent months, the press has once again denounced the situation there on several occasions, praising the effort the National Parks have made without government support. Álvaro launched several campaigns, showcasing the "agony of Corcovado" at the hands of outlaws. But the sensitivities of the Government are in other spheres of power. At the end of the day, Corcovado will not win them more votes when the fast-approaching elections finally arrive. That's what matters to them.

Álvaro has won the war at last, battle by battle, trench by trench. He has had epic endurance, but he has finally cleared Corcovado of gold miners. With the collaboration between the park rangers and the local police they have not subsided until every last one was evicted. There were no less than three hundred and fifty families inside the park. Hopefully this time it will be definitive, as it has been an eleven-year battle against destruction. You and I know that devastation is quick. The full restoration of life is a much slower cycle.

Today the Nicaraguans are revved up, launching fireworks into the air. Reina arrived happy because the International Court of Justice has ruled that the United States is guilty and must pay Nicaragua for supporting the Contras. They don't know how much, but they are already speculating about what their government will do with the money. They think they are going to share it with the population. They are naïve because things don't work like that in politics. Losses are socialized, but profits line anonymous pockets.

Olof, I think I forgot to tell you that Patricia was pregnant again. She has had a girl who was born at a friend's house in Santa Ana three days ago. Her name will be Syska. They're both doing well, from what she told me on the phone. This time I haven't been able to go see her in Santa Ana, because my cabins are full of tourists. I am so excited for them to come back home any time now, I expect it could be them in every car I hear coming down the street.

1987

I haven't written to you in a long time, Olof. Time passes by and I don't even realize it. I keep myself very entertained with Patricia's two children. I spend a lot of time with them because I enjoy being a grandmother. I can't compete with their energy, however, and by nightfall I feel tired, and it is at night that I like to write because no one interrupts me.

Sometimes I think it's better not to be up to date on current events. Today I went to see the cobbler from Cóbano, Don Gustavo, whose shop is located in front of the airfield, and I brought him several sandals to be repair. While I waited, I browsed through a newspaper from a week ago, one of those old ones he keeps on the counter and uses to wrap repaired shoes.

One of the articles brings news from Ecuador. There have been two earthquakes measuring 6.1 and 6.9 on the Richter scale. They left more than a thousand dead. I think this is a young continent and it is still settling in, looking for its place. Here people get very scared when they get news of earthquakes in other latitudes. Because they know that this is a country with great seismic activity, due to the friction between the Cocos and Caribbean plates. It is the phenomenon most feared by the population because it is impossible to foresee. The earthquake in 1983, on the Osa Peninsula, left long lasting repercussions among the population.

The cobbler has a granddaughter who sat next to me while I read. With a very serious look she asked if I needed someone to work at the cabins. I asked her who the job was for and she responded it was for her. She was barely ten years old, imagine! I told her that she had to go to school and that when he finished studying, she would have a better job than the one I could offer in the cabins. Grandpa didn't know about our conversation, but he handed her the sandals and she wrapped them up for me with a skill that amazed me. As I left her, she came to the door and asked me not to forget about her because she needed the job. She shouted that her name is Dunia, as I walked out.

It is already December and Montezuma is filling up with tourists who arrive by bus and by boat. This afternoon a Belgian has arrived. She is a woman in her forties, with exquisite manners. She arrived alone, with a very elegant little travel bag. Reina was already gone and I was feeding the cats when she peered into the patio. She asked me with surprise if I cooked for all those cats. I answered yes, that I cooked for my cats and sometimes for other two-legged animals as well. Fortunately for both of us, she took it as a joke and waited patiently until the end of the feeding hour to ask for a room. More and more women are traveling alone to escape from their lives. Yes, it seems that the life of couples is also becoming "disposable". Although I don't know anything about her life, if this beautiful and educated woman is still single it must be by choice. She will stay for a week.

She brought Marguerite Yourcenar's book *Oriental Tales*, which I had borrowed from the Humlegarden library. She told me that the author had just passed away, in Maine, United States, and she was rereading it in posthumous tribute. Her name is Grace, just like Marguerite's partner. There are curious synchronisms.

Today I learned that it is not just a synchronism. Grace told me that her mother and Margarita's Grace were childhood friends and corresponded for years. When she found out that she was pregnant, she asked her to name the child after her, because she knew that she would have no offspring. I came to tell you as soon as she left for her room in case I forget. It's not that it's important, but I had a hunch that the name was not a coincidence. And so it is, it is a causality.

The year is ending and the cabins are full, so much so that I have rented my room and for a few days I will sleep on a bench under an almond tree in the patio. I have to raise the money to pay the taxes on the farm and the cabins.

1988

It is March, Olof, and everything is so dry again. As soon as I catch a scent of smoke, I am overtaken by thoughts of fire. I even wake up dreaming of fire sometimes. I am obsessed with it and we are still two months away from the rains. The riverbeds are dry and full of stones. The sight of bushes and trees scorched by the sun and the parched ravines saddens me. I think the seasons get more extreme as the years go by. I don't remember such scorching heat when we arrived as there is now. People say that the sea used to be much rougher, however, that in winter the swell washed away the little houses that were near the beach.

I've been roaming the woods on my way to visit you. The mangoes have grown much, I think that in a month or so they will be ready to collect. Today I have some beautiful, fragrant papayas for the smoothies. Unfortunately, the medlars are running out, but the harvest was abundant, as were the star apples, which have grown tremendously. They are imposing trees, just like the mangos, full of amazing foliage. I feel so small when I stand beside them.

This October the entire country was on edge due to Hurricane Juana. The press had terrified the inhabitants of Limón for an entire week, and they evacuated the coastal area days before the expected arrival. The buses were filled, and when there was no more space, people walked inland, carrying their lives in a few swollen bags.

But the forecasts were wrong. Instead, the hurricane winds and the corresponding deluges affected the Southern Pacific zone, causing several deaths and destroying homes, crops, and livestock. The houses built on riverbanks floated out like pleasure rafts, equipped for a long excursion. Juana's sudden change of course caught the authorities, the Emergency Committee, and the population off guard. All eyes and contingency plans were directed towards Limón, and nothing happened there.

Fortunately, here we only got torrential rain for several days, as befits the seasonal weather in October. But Bluefields, on the Atlantic coast of Nicaragua, suffered the worst damage. The ocean rose and hit the coasts with gigantic waves that took hundreds of people and devastated the coastal towns, which have had to start rebuilding from the ground up. When nature gets angry, we can only make ourselves even more insignificant and take cover.

On one occasion a storm caused me to panic. It was in October 1969. You had left for Montezuma to deliver some letters to the post office and buy batteries for the record player and the flashlight. It started to rain but you said it was insignificant, because when you had decided to go there was no way you were going to change your mind. But when it had been raining torrentially for several hours and the thunder made the mountain rumble, night fell and you still had not returned. I went outside illuminated by lightning, which drew maps in the sky. I couldn't continue, however, because it was high tide and the sea was threatening to overtake the path to the beach. I spent the night sitting in the room by candlelight.

The next day you told me that the Colorado River was so swollen with water that it could not be crossed, no matter how hard you tried. You had to return to town and spend the night at the police post. You couldn't cross until 9:00 the next morning. When I saw you appear, I felt my life turn on again. Living here meant that anything could happen, but the full acceptance of this consequence was not immediate. A maturation time was needed.

This morning Joaquín returned from attending the last meeting of the year in San José. He had a serious face and a newspaper with the news of the assassination of the Brazilian ecologist Chico Mendes, the defender of the Amazon and its native tribes. His messages were truths that struck people on the face like a fist:

"Don't sell the land. When you transform it into money, you lose the possibility of survival. The land is life."

It was like hearing you, when you took that walk to Tambor advising the locals not to sell their land. No wonder they killed him. His truths annoyed his killers, I'm sure of it. The culprits are a landowner and his son who will be sentenced to nineteen years in prison. I doubt very much that the sentence will be carried out, but the motive and the murderers have been identified. That stigma will be carried on by their descendants in the coming generations. Chico was another victim of greed, and ignorance, just like you. He knew that sooner or later he would be eliminated. One of his messages is written on the epitaph: *I don't want flowers on my grave because I know they will be picked from the forest.* And so it has been, not a single flower has been laid on his grave. Consistent to the end. I am sure that he will patrol the Amazon from some eternal place, beyond the clouds.

It was then that I understood Joaquín's sorrowful gesture. He also walks the tightrope of wildlife conservation. Totally unprotected. It is a tragic paradox that the act of protecting another, leaves you unprotected. Because he does it with such determination does not mean that he ignores the risks that threaten him. The problem with heroes is that they are ordinary people, with nothing to save them, not even from themselves and their dogmas.

Another year that does not end well.

Karen Mogensen and Joaquín Alvarado in Cabo Blanco

Part Three

El Sano Banano

1989

*T*he opening of Patricia and Lenny's restaurant has caused a real stir, altering the daily texture of town life. They have named it El Sano Banano, The Healthy Banana. They bake every day, and it is truly changing the diets of our neighbors, although most of their clientele are tourists or foreign residents who are accustomed to the flavors and varieties of other cuisines. The first few days, when they began testing recipes, the aromas of nutmeg, cinnamon, and walnuts emerged from their oven. People stopped in front of the store, as if they were floating on the breath of the aroma.

I watched them spellbound, and their gestures reminded me of *Babette's Feast*. Once again, Karen Blixen helped me understand the keys to the world and the unquestionable fact that "food was no longer just a matter of eating so as not to perish. It had to satisfy the palate of those who had the money to buy it." Scent stimulates the taste buds, that cannot be denied, and people are moved by sensations that reach our brain and push us towards one decision or another.

Yes, as Karen Blixen said, food changes people's nature and behavior. Just look at the Mantled Howlers, they are so peaceful, feeding mostly on leaves. White-faced Capuchins, however, are omnivores and eat meat if they can catch it. That is why they are more combative. It's no secret, we most certainly are what we eat.

And do you know who is working at El Sano Banano? Dunia, that little girl from the cobbler, the shoemaker's granddaughter. There are people who rise early to accomplish their vital objectives.

The first schoolteacher that I remember from this area was already here when we arrived, his name was Isidro. He was just a boy who hadn't even turned eighteen. He came to the little school in Mal País to substitute the previous teacher, who was on maternity leave. He was a small, serene boy, willing to teach a handful of students, some of whom were bigger than he was. He told us that some parents did not want to accept someone so young. It seemed to them that he did not meet the indispensable conditions of knowledge and respect that he had to impose on their children. But the students requested that he remain and he finally stayed until the end of the school year in December.

We often spoke about the importance of emphasizing the need to protect the forest to the children. Unfortunately, he only stayed that year, because of the many difficulties and risks of living here without the shelter of family. The school was a little ranch with a wooden floor, on the edge of the jungle. Since there was no way to give him accommodation, they built a loft for him in the school itself. So, he had his home and his work all in the same room. One day, visibly shocked, he told us that he had found a shed skin of a Fer-de-lance Pit Viper where he slept. For a city boy, it was difficult to accept this "normal" jungle event.

At that time the teacher could barely glimpse what life would be like in the future. Neither he nor anyone else could imagine where our materialistic culture was headed. Where will children learn to take care of our common home if they do not teach it in schools? Who will care for this most valuable and essential resource on which the continuity of our species depends? The world is changing at an unprecedented speed, and I reflect once again on the fact that public property is often only used to reap material benefits. But when it comes to protecting it for conservation, few feel the call to fulfill this responsibility. Natural resources do not belong to men, but to the land itself. Appropriating them to sustain life is not a codified universal law, yet it is obeyed by our ancestors. If we do not respect the rights of the land itself, who or what will sustain life? What criteria will determine which creatures perish and which continue to exist? Who will guard of our common heritage? When the children pass by, on their way to school, I stop to observe them and try to find a sign of sensitivity. I look for something that manifests their intention to continue our task, yours, mine, and that of the park rangers. It is essential to fulfill the correspondence and symbiosis between the earth and its inhabitants. As the indigenous say: we are not producers, only caretakers. The earth is the only producer.

***

We are already at Christmas again. The breaking wind makes people resonate it, like a message delivered by a chain of good resolutions. At first it was hard for you and I to understand. Why would the wind make people think about Christmas? We always wondered in the early years, when we heard people repeat it daily. But then we realized that the wind of this season is light, cheerful and arrives after the rains, relieving submerged moods.

The breeze that shakes the palm trees gradually intensifies and carries the aroma of tamales from one house to the next, to the next, and beyond. The whole town smells like Christmas. Women spend entire days preparing the dough with corn flour. They mix the dough with various types of meat, vegetables, and spices, then they wrap it with banana leaves. On Christmas Eve and Christmas Day, family and friends then embark on a pilgrimage from house to house to wish each other peace. It's such a different tradition than what we had in Europe. Although our European tradition is well perceived, perhaps it is not so much. Sweets and cookies were prepared there with the same intention of entertaining, and I suppose that here too there will be more than one brother-in-law or cousin who will not be welcomed in some homes. The extreme friendliness that the Ticos display and the absence of critical capacity are two traits that they do not share with Europe, however, which is so advanced and cold. So, a warm welcome and a tamal are guaranteed to all this time of year. Life is getting lighter, albeit eventually.

My cabins are bursting with people. There is almost no time to wash the sheets and towels of departing guests before the next guests have already arrived. Every day people arrive asking if any rooms are available. The town is growing as tourism increases. There are more and more constructions, like mushrooms that sprout after the rain. Fortunately, there is not much room to grow, because of the shape of this town, nestled between the base of the mountain and the sea, so it can never be very big. The road is still dirt, and the trip here is as long as a day without water. But people continue to arrive, especially young people, who carry their meager luggage in a backpack. It takes little to live here if you have the will to do it. I have rented my room so these days I sleep on the bench under the almond tree. Taxes rule.

***

I don't know the whole story, but Pablo came to bring me some vegetarian tamales which Nery sent me, and he told me that the US Army had just invaded Panama. He says that he has seen gunfire and bombs flying in all directions on television. I don't like this news. We are too close to Panama and it will affect Costa Rica in some way if they do not resolve the war that they have just declared soon.

Events that affect people's lives in a shocking way always occur when we get to the end of the year, like a New Year resolution, like bringing one way of life to a close in order to start a new one. But we have run out of time for anything else to happen, because today is the 31st. As I write to you, I can hear the noise of the tourists and the crash of beer bottles, toasting in various languages while they dance in the middle of the street. Pachanga music began at noon and has been increasing, in volume and the intensity of the repertoire, from swing to cumbia, playing in the shops where they sell beer.

There is one hour left before they light the fireworks and hug each other in that irrational apotheosis. All the excesses, including the amount of alcohol ingested and the inevitable hangover, will prevent them from getting out of bed tomorrow because their body weighs them down.

I will retreat to my little bench now, although the thunder of the fireworks will surely wake me when twelve o'clock arrives. It's another year without you, but also without sadness. Little by little it has left me. Now I enjoy what life brings me. I will also toast, for the two of us.

1990

I was sitting so comfortably in the patio on New Year's Day, exchanging cuddles with my favorite cat *Mis-mis* on my lap, when John came to tell me that Nelson Mandela had been released from a South African prison after twenty-seven years. He told it matter-of-factly, with his hands in his pockets, in that gesture which is so typical in him. He has been robbed of the best years of his life. If I had to choose between being in jail or being dead, I would prefer the latter. No person can remain unchanged after so many years locked up and tortured. Although we are not what we were after twenty-seven years in freedom either. It takes strength and an iron will to stay alive when there is no stimulus for existence, and from what he has shown, Mandela has both.

John also told me that the cost of asphalting the slope on the entrance to town has been budgeted, since last winter the path was severed several times due to the rains. He is a good neighbor who consistently contributes to the betterment of our town. On the one hand, it is very necessary, so as not to be isolated. On the other, I know this means that more cars and more people will arrive, which is not so desirable. Progress and its contradictions.

***

I have been telling you that many Nicaraguans have been settling throughout Costa Rica and have also arrived here, because there is work in construction, in hotels and restaurants. They always have the same strategy: one of them arrives and settles and then calls other relatives. They arrive with their eyes wide open from what they have seen and suffered in their own country. Their highest aspiration is to find a job that allows them to live in peace. They accept anything. They are hard-working and brave people, but they are tired of so many years of war. It is not surprising. They fled from the war and famine caused by their dictator and the conspiracy of the United States and its imperialism, whose arrogance has made them believe that all of America is their territory, from north to south. They act as if these countries are their backyard and they can carry out abuses without generating complains. They impose and depose rulers as they please. The exodus of men and women from Nicaragua, El Salvador and even Honduras does not stop. It will take many years to restore peace and life in communities where both sides can coexist in all of these countries.

A woman has just won the presidential elections in Nicaragua and today Reina was very happy when she arrived. She believes that having a woman in charge will prevent more wars in her country, and she may be right. Because women do not wage war, although they do not allow us to forge peace either.

***

What a fright we had yesterday, Olof! It seemed that the great earthquake of the Nicoya peninsula, which they have predicted for years, had finally arrived. We learned later that the magnitude was a seven on the Richter scale and the epicenter was in Cóbano. It was seven in the morning and I was preparing a hibiscus smoothie for a tourist who is breathing badly due to a mucus problem. With the noise of the blender, I didn't feel the dragging sound that precedes the shaking. But instantly, the floor undulated like a snake and all the knick-knacks in the kitchen fell down with a crash. Many houses in Cóbano and the entire area, including Montezuma, suffered significant damage. It was nothing less than general panic. Many foreigners who travel here have been asking about the great earthquake in the Nicoya Peninsula for a few years now.

The Cocos plate has been a threat since US researchers published it, alerting the population of their own country to take the precaution of not traveling to this area. The risk was the same before the publication, but nobody suffered from what might happen; neither they nor we felt that we were in danger. But sometimes it is data that conditions our lives. Although they are mere hypotheses and these dire forecasts never come to pass.

People are anguished about something that exists only in thought. Tell me if we're not ridiculous.

The old people of the town recalled yesterday that the last great earthquake in Nicoya was in 1950 and it was felt from Santa Cruz to Cabo Blanco. Those who were children back then, told stories of how the tide rose and left many fish on the shore. Although some claimed that did not happen from the earthquake, but from some very strong tides thirty years ago instead. Because of the tremor we got to listen to different stories all with different versions, like when we first arrived and people gathered at the end of the day. Once again, I think that everything has a purpose, if you know how to find it.

As for the earthquake, experts believe that the risk is based on the accumulation of a large amount of energy in the area of friction, and that sooner or later it will explode. They consider that the greatest danger would be the formation of a giant wave. The houses that are on the seashore, which is most of this town, would be engulfed by the unleashed power of the sea. But who knows if it will ever go beyond a simple shudder. People die every day of everyday things. They die in their own beds but that doesn't stop them from going to bed. I sincerely believe that there are so many ways to lose your life, that it is not worth worrying about any one of them. Although I was scared at first, afterwards I went about my life as if nothing had happened. When night came, I slept in my bed like a rock, so soundly that I don't remember that night's dreams.

***

We are in the month of May and some journalists and cameramen have arrived to interview me for Danish television. I invited them into the courtyard once the shock wore off. They said the program will be broadcast on Channel 2. They asked me questions and I emptied my wealth of memories for nearly five hours. We were often interrupted, as always happens around here. I told them about why we had to get to Moctezuma and all the events that have happened since then. I also spoke about your murder. Sometimes that word is so hard for me that I would like to change it for a kinder one, but I immediately regret it. I feel that I betray the veracity of the facts by changing it, and your memory has been betrayed too many times already for me to be part of that game. You were murdered and we will never know the whole truth, even if that doesn't matter anymore.

Since your one-way trip to Corcovado, I cannot count how many times I've repeated the reasons that brought us here and sometimes I grow tired of retelling the story. On the other hand, it is an opportunity to speak about you again, about us. I have the chance to relive, even if it is only for a few hours, what life was like with you when I answer their questions. Before it hurt me to talk about it, but not anymore.

One must adapt to living among the accumulated rubble of a life in constant construction. We must understand that sadness has to be loved, the same way as joy, because both are feelings that belong to us and make us who we are. It is our true legacy.

Before leaving, the journalists recorded images of the beach as I walked along the shore and waved goodbye to them. They left with much gratitude and a big smile. On the one hand, I wanted to finish telling the story so they would let me rest. On the other hand, I felt happy to be able to speak in my mother tongue about you, about us. I felt renewed inside.

The Television

Madremonte, "Mother of the forest". That's what the journalist María Isabel Casas called me at the beginning of the interview for the magazine. She was interested in learning about the profound changes that had taken place in the farming community of Montezuma hich had led the families to a continuous exodus towards the capital.

Madremonte. What a nice definition. She moved me and flattered me, although I rather consider myself a daughter of nature.

"The problem," I explained, remembering your words "was that the land was depleted due to misuse and contamination. It no longer produced as it did at first, because the land was exhausted and the water was poisoned by the agrochemicals. So, the farmers began to sell out and they brought in the cattle and that ended everything." The cattle, those poor animals, are exploited until the end of their lives, they harness everything and thank them for nothing. First, they take the milk; when their udders dry up, they take their meat; and finally, their skin, tendons, and bones. They meet an atrocious death at the end of their days. They are crammed in trucks with many others, shaking as they ramble down the road. Dirty, thirsty, and frightened, they are handed over to the butchers, who dismember them before they are completely dead.

I don't know how anyone can think that such battered meat can be good for our stomachs. This is how, I am convinced, we contract the fears and illnesses that lead us to premature death. We traded forests full of trees and life, for bad pastures to maintain sad cattle. So much grass and so much water is needed to produce a meat product that is not a mainstay in the diet of the native population, because Ticos barely eat meat, but it is devoured abroad. To top it off, the grasses that the cattle eat are contaminated with pesticides and insecticides. The more meat they eat, the more poisoned they become. If our diet were based on grains, with the same expenditure of resources, we could feed a multiplied population. That is provable, with data, but no one cares about data.

Families began migrating to San José in the nineteen-seventies, looking for work in factories and changing their lifestyle and the population of the town decreased. It was a painful exodus, I told her. Watching our neighbors leaving on the boat, which travelled twice per week. Entire families, with elderly and children, not quite knowing how they were going to live or what they were going to live on. They fled from a self-imposed scarcity brought on by depleting and annihilating the land.

The goodbye scenes were dramatic, and I suffered on each occasion that I had to witness them. The twenty houses that made up the town of Montezuma became uninhabited. The lights went out one after another, and only the echo of absent voices resonated. Montezuma's dream had turned into a daily nightmare, without any remedy to stop it. This town was very small then, it looked a lot like a ghost town. People who arrived in town did not even realize they were already in it. After turning the last curve, they were suddenly in the center of town. If they didn't stop walking, their feet would quickly reach the sand on the beach and take them into the sea.

The song churned out by the axels of the ox carts was also silenced. They no longer passed by complaining, bleeding out their bores with a sound reminiscent of conch shells and cambutes. More than eighty pairs of oxen locked by the yoke came together on fair days. The farmers arrived herding their pigs from Río Frío de Arío, more than ten hours of travel. Everything was sold and bought in that fair of prodigious and abundant merchandise.

If the footsteps of the oxen, heavy and massive on the dirt road, were silent it was because there were no longer sacks of corn, rice, or beans to carry to the boat. Market days, Monday and Thursday, were reduced to one and later to none. And so, little by little, Montezuma's life faded away, burning out like a candle.

If we analyze the reasons, we reach the same conclusion, again and again: poor education. This was the source of the problem. There was nowhere for them to train here, except for the school, which was deficient. Almost no one completed the statutory years because they did not value their studies. It was said that they didn't need to go to school to cut grass, but there was no grass to cut when they arrived at the companies. The bosses in San José were very demanding and the old farmers were unfamiliar with "efficient" labor, which their bosses grew weary of repeating over and over.

By the time the migrant families realized that life in the capital was very difficult and that they had a miserable lifestyle, in the so-called marginal neighborhoods, it was already too late. They no longer had a house or land anywhere, and they had to stay there. Some with degrading and poorly paid jobs, others begging, and some committing crimes or selling their bodies. It was terrible and devastating, especially for those who got involved in drug trafficking. It was a momentary escape from the misery, but they didn't know that you can't run away forever. At some point we have to stop and face the consequences of our actions.

Television was much to blame, by promoting a model of life that brings so much harm to us with its programs. Many families did not have electricity, like us, but when they began to sell the land to tourists, they did not know what to do with the money. It seemed to them that the money would never run out, and they spent it like water running through their fingers. I remember what Frank told us one afternoon when he came to bring us a wounded horse. A family from Mal País had sold a farm and went to Puntarenas to see what they could buy with the money, they had to get rid of it as if it were burning their hands. They were amazed to see how the water was kept cool in the refrigerator, so they brought a large one for their house. The refrigerator was divided into many compartments for fruits, eggs, and vegetables. When they got it to their house, they realized that it was powered by electricity and they didn't have any. Well, we never knew if it was true or not, because Frank was quite the joker.

The television brought lies, and the lies were transformed in their heads into false realities. They did not know this, however, and the television quickly gained credibility and ranked as the Court of Truth. People said: "That's true, because it was on the television." As if it were the word of their god. Women and men with perfect aesthetics, as if rendered by an artist, appeared on the screens. They lived in houses of unimaginable and excessive luxury and drove brightly colored cars through streets lined with gardens and shopping malls where you could buy everything, the useful and the useless, the essential and the illusory. The latter is what captured their attention and became part of an obsession in their emotional universe: they would spare no expense to acquire it. The television could be the most wonderful tool for education, but it is at the service of capitalism and consumerism, our worst enemies. Both are the biggest source of unhappiness in the world.

The day Benjamín, a Montezuma resident, brought the television to town it was the prelude to a cultural disaster. Before that day, people lived happily in their ranches on the edge of the beach. Every day at nightfall they would gather outside, warming up tortillas and drinking raw milk. Whoever passed by, native or foreign, was welcome and invited to the gathering. Jokes and ghost stories were told. The story of a girl dressed as a bride was always included, with her white dress, her flower crown and tulle and even a bouquet of flowers in her hand, on some days they were jasmine and on others white roses.

She rested her back on a palm tree when night fell, looking for her missing husband and drawing men in with her eyes. They told other stories of mythological beings, such as Cadejos, La Llorona, and La Cegua. We could listen to the same stories a thousand times because each narrator added a new ingredient, making it unique.

Sometimes the various narrators argued: if the legend was true, if she had appeared to this or that neighbor, if it the apparition happened on a bend in the road or in the meanders of the river, if she was fully clothed or almost naked, and if her face was in a grimace of pain or if she had a beautiful face streaked with tears. Some said that she cried and others that she sang a melody so sad it soured the milk in the pitchers. It depended, above all, on the character of the narrator. But it all ended with laughter and wishes of good night and see you tomorrow. Oh, how we laughed like chachalacas, our whole body shaking from that healthy energy generated by laughter.

But that ominous day, the exodus began, although at that time we could not foresee it. The first symptom from the neighbors was an unusual rush, they did not stop to greet us. I thought that perhaps we were going back to the problems we had when we first arrived, when they would gossip about our misdeeds, which is how our fight to protect the forest was interpreted. I even thought that perhaps we misunderstood their attitudes, due to our ignorance of their customs.

I mentioned it to you worried, as we walked to the post office. We learned the reason for the rush when we arrived at the center of Montezuma. Benjamín had set up some long benches for the first television session, twenty-five cents per viewer. The device was on a high shelf, inside the police station, and the benches were on the street. It worked thanks to the only generator in town, which was his. He was a businessman, more of a visionary than most of the neighbors, but also compassionate when people asked him for help.

The unwise consequence of his venture was that there were no more gatherings; his majesty the television had arrived and they watched it hypnotized, conceding to it the best moments of their lives: the time when work was over in which they took stock of what the day left them. It was a magical hour devoted to the gathering of families and neighbors; the moment to vent worries, share daily events and to quantify the toll life takes on us all. In those shared moments, the load seemed lighter, because the burden was shared by everyone. Those were also moments of consultations and recommendations about problems with sowing or the harvest; perhaps even about an ailment that could be cured with their knowledge of plants, roots, and spells.

They stopped going to bed like the chickens, respecting the cycle that marked the rhythm of their harmonized existence as farmers. They stayed until eleven or twelve at night, caught up in the screen and held spellbound by the television. Watching soap operas that arrived from other countries, arguing with the characters, as if they were real and could respond to their challenges.

The football came somewhat later. Football games and their players were occupying a bigger space in their lives than the members of their own family. When electricity was installed in town, the first thing they bought was a television, thereby bringing the enemy into the house. No other appliance had or will have that power, anywhere in the world.

Neighborhood life as we knew it ended then. The gatherings in the cool of the night, the placidly light chats or the discussion of serious matters that concerned us all and solving community problems with the complicity of the serene and calm night are over.

Benjamin had unknowingly introduced the enemy of the community, which surreptitiously stole our model of life. Of course, if Benjamin hadn't brought the television, it would have arrived anyway, hand in hand with that supposed prosperity and modernity. Yes, television stole their lives and identity. Nothing was ever the same again.

They were told how to live their lives from every angle, without room for reflection and freedom. Television had a credibility that cast doubt upon the reality of their traditional model of life. The simple fact that something appeared on the screen certified it as authentic, even if it was a lie as big as Chirripó.

It remains like that today. In all areas, culture, politics, business and even traditions, which are invented from one day to the next and are considered traditions from that moment on. Now, watching television in the homes of families is a nightly tradition. The label of tradition seems to cover everything with honor, despite the abundance of despicable and hateful traditions. One appalling example is the "droit de seigneur", nothing more than a barbarous abuse of authority, which granted feudal lords the right to sexual relations with maidens who married their servants.

This makes me think that words and their meanings set traps for us. People must recognize the words and observe them, through the distance granted by elapsed time. Therefore, old age should contain wisdom and keep people away from that screen.

That old joke came to mind, the one about the Indians who were collecting firewood for the winter. Their shaman told them it would be a very cold winter, but the reality is that he did not know. He was young and had received a modern education in a university outside the reservation. So, he got on the phone with the capital's weather service, which told him yes, it would be a cold winter. When he asked what the indications were for this forecast, the meteorologist responded that the Indians were hoarding firewood, and the Indian's knowledge of the climate was beyond all doubt and discussion.

María Isabel Casas laughed heartily when I told her this story, but so many things are like that in our culture. We need each other to survive and all knowledge is useful for the purpose of survival.

I believe that human arrogance is the biggest problem. We think that we are superior to other animals, despite the evidence that we are not. You need look no further than the fact that we are the only species that threatens its own habitat. No other living being is so barbarous. Nobody chooses their own destruction, except us. "Observe the little birds," I told María Isabel, "They can walk, swim, fly, build their nests and raise their children, naturally, without giving themselves any importance. They do not have to pretend to be anything they are not to anyone."

"Look," I told her, "During the first few years after we arrived many baby White-faced Capuchins came to our ranch. They had cut down the forest and hunted their mothers, they didn't have a place where they felt protected. Sometimes they fought among themselves, because they are very territorial and at that time the only place where they felt protected was our farm. During those years the population did not increase. No baby monkeys to be found. But when we bought the farm adjoining ours, they understood that they could reproduce, and babies were born again."

"The animals understood that in a situation of territorial or food crisis, they should not contribute to increasing the problem. Humana beings, however, don't perceive this. In this area, there are families with twenty-four and twenty-six children, despite scarcity and precarious living. Tell me if we humans have anything to brag about? As my German teacher used to say, back in Copenhagen, "Even the gods are futilely fighting against the stupidity of men." I think it is a matter of will, and will must be reinforced daily, it is not something that comes naturally."

She looked at me thoughtfully as she picked up the tape recorder. When she was leaving, she told me that she thought I lived according to my principles and the impulse of nature, because they were both integrated. This girl's opinion was very nice and that night I went to sleep thinking about her. Some comforting events make me reconcile with the human species.

Karen in front of her cabins in Montezuma

A visit from Eva Tellow

Olof, after so many letters with the promise of a visit, your niece Eva is finally coming. Thirty-six years have passed since I have seen anyone from our families, that is almost ten more years than my age when we left Europe. I have spent more years of my life here than in Denmark. How can I not consider myself Costa Rican?

She says that he will arrive in two weeks with her children, Peter and Karolina, and some friends of theirs. It's great news, don't you think? The first visit from members of our family in all these years. I'm glad they're coming, but I don't know if they'll be able to live here, not even for two weeks. The countryside is not a comfortable place for people from cities. I can't stand life in the city, I suffocate when I have to go to San José. The hours I spend there seem to last longer than sixty minutes.

I can't hide the fact that I'm excited. I know that your father sent some photos, but I can't find them now that I'm looking for them. Of course, so many years have passed that it would be impossible to recognize her. But it will not be difficult to find them in Montezuma as there are not so many tourists in August.

They finally arrived yesterday, August 12, exhausted from the trip. They did the last leg of the journey, from the pier in Paquera to Montezuma, in a cattle truck. I was waiting for them in

Montezuma and then I put them up in Cocalito. I felt sorry for them when I saw them, I couldn't tell if they were more tired or scared. They slept almost ten hours straight.

The next morning they enjoyed the sea and the sun. I warned them of the danger of sunstroke, but at the end of the day their faces were red and full of freckles, as if they had sunbathed with a sieve. Peter's face and messy hair, so blond, almost white, reminded me so much of yours...

None of them said it, but I think our simple way of living has caused an impression on them. They might not have the words to express it without hurting my feelings. Yes, I guess it's hard to imagine life here coming from a city in the civilized world, with all the resources you think you need at your fingertips, and the money to buy them.

At night we talked and talked, especially Eva and I. I feel great joy and relief to have someone that I can talk to about you, as if somehow, through words I could touch you. She tells me, evoking a warm and fun tone, things from your childhood that have been passed down within the family. She also told of other times she shared with you when her mother, Hilde, passed away, although she was very young at the time. You were always the strange one in the family. The manias with vegetarian food and your compassion for the suffering of street animals were not common at the time. They also didn't understand why you gave up your military career to farm the land in Speleby.

I told her how we met, although she knew the story, and I felt an exquisite pleasure in my mouth and great emotion through my entire being, as I named the locations we shared and my sudden infatuation, which occurred spontaneously the moment I laid eyes on you. I told her about our trip, beginning when we set sail in May 1954 on the *Astrid Bakke*. I continued with our travels in Central America and our arrival here, and her gestures shifted from looks of compassion to astonishment.

She had seen pictures of the two of us and I know she found me old and wrinkled, my hair colored in two tones: gray and white. The spots and wrinkles on my hands and face bear the evidence of hours of sunshine, but they reflect the wounds of my daily existence. Photos don't age, but people do... and I don't know how to perform that Dorian Gray trick, which allowed him to stay young, while his portrait aged.

The other problem is that the alternative to aging is not very suggestive or desirable, although you know that at one point I considered it my best option. In the past, I have sometimes wondered if it takes more courage to die or to continue living. But for years I have been satisfied with what life has brought me. I'm not satisfied, however, with what it took from me: you.

Eva asked me repeatedly while she was here if I wasn't afraid of the animals, not even jaguars, because on the boat trip they met a foreigner who told them they were reproducing. I wish it were true.

Imagine when they saw the coatis make their entrance. Once again, I saw that mixture of fear and curiosity on their faces. Although they had seen photos of *Lis*, but of course it is never the same as seeing them live.

Everyone tried the pochote leaf smoothie at breakfast and there were all kinds of opinions, but I think it's not their favorite food. I can't blame them, it takes some getting used to.

I recounted with the same pain as always, the details of your death and my misgivings about the reasons. To this day, I still think that the interests of the banana and citrus companies, or the loggers, had something to do with it. Even gold panners were suspect to me, and I told her so. I didn't tell her about my tormented visit to the Puntarenas prison to ask the murderer why he had killed you. It was useless to frighten her further.

With a mix of affection and sadness Eva reminded me of the great displeasure felt by your father, "Grandpa Hugo", she called him. She pointed out, gently, that he never got over our departure. Sometimes, when the pain of your absence hurt him more than he could bear, he would say to her contemptuously: "My son Olle has chosen to go live with the monkeys, from tree to tree, and it seems that he will never return." He would stand up and leave after saying it so no one would see his tears. He used his last words to utter your name with a resigned sigh when he passed away, that's what Eva told me. He was very weak. He had been deteriorating and when the day of the operation came, he didn't have the heart to continue living. Then, the post operation period was complicated, and he could not overcome it. She believed that was why he passed on, he simply didn't want to go on living.

I wanted to ask her about the reasons why no members of the family accompanied me at your funeral, especially because of the tragic circumstances of your death. When the question was on the tip of my tongue, I thought better of it and preferred not to stir up a painful sore. What use would it be for me to understand now? Since you have been gone, you know, I decided to accept what life gives me in the doses it deems appropriate.

She did not hold back, however. She asked me if we had tried to have children after my abortion, when I fell off the bicycle in Speleby. Remembering it saddened me deeply. If we had had a son, he would be an extension of you and I had thought about it countless times after your death, during my days of profound loneliness. I told her no, that I could never get pregnant again. I recited to her, my voice trembling with emotion, the poetry of the pianist Jelly Roll Morton to reveal my true and deepest feelings:

Every time the changin' of the moon,

The blood come rushin' from the bitch's womb...

We were in the corridor, as we were every night, and the boys played on the beach while the moonlight spilled over the earth. *Lis* approached us and seeing I was sad, she gave me a piece of papaya, waiting for my smile. Eva couldn't believe that the coati understood my emotions and was impressed by the evidence.

She was also struck by the fact that *Lis* had a bandaged leg and did not rip the bandage off. I put it on because she had an infected wound and was walking with great difficulty. I had to accompany her the past few days so she would walk slowly. She didn't want to sit still, naturally, so I had to do more walks in the woods than usual. We walked more than three hours a day, following the routes that she usually travels. Humans do not realize that the life of animals is a full-time occupation. They don't have to arrive at an exact time for work, but looking for sustenance, mating, and raising their cubs is as laborious as it is in our lives. The difference is that if an animal cannot to sustain its life, it perishes. They don't have a mother or father to do things for them when they are adults. I think that is the essence of personal responsibility. Nature cannot permit irresponsibility.

When I went to bed, I reflected on accepting loss. Mastering the difficult science of losing, without leaving a negative stain on life, is a slow-brewed lesson. Yes, living is definitely an artform, an exercise that is learned as we construct our life.

It is comforting when you discover that any piece of organic or inorganic matter can have a new life, be reborn as part of something different. To think that nothing is lost forever; it lays at rest somewhere, awaiting reunion.

It is like collecting part of the old life to form something new and unknown. You decipher with certainty that in another time and place you were part of something that was and ceased to be, to end up shaping what you are now. And the process is repeated over and over again, in imperceptible harmony, as part of the dynamics of life. Because I believe, conclusively, that "Nothing changes, but everything is transformed", as Heraclitus, the wisest among the Greek philosophers, said so many centuries ago.

Yesterday, when I was coming back from visiting you, Eva asked me where you were buried. I told her that it was on the hill, but that it was our bastion and no one but me could get near it. I think she had been watching me, but I know she respects my privacy. Before going to bed she hugged me more intensely than other days.

They left this morning. I accompanied them to Montezuma early in the morning and walked back with the pleasant sensation of being in charge of my own time, even though their company has pleased me these days and made me happy. Someone said that visitors are like rain: "so much joy when they arrive, and so much relief when they leave". My life is back to normal and in two days their lives will return to normal too. This is how it should be: live and let live. They have many new experiences to talk about.

A Costa Rican in Sweden

*J*oaquín is going to Stockholm. How about? His goal is to raise funds to expand the limits of the Reserve and improve surveillance. The resources sent by the Government through National Parks are insufficient for the essential maintenance of the Reserve. As Carlos says, here "we work tooth and nail, because we have had our teeth and nails from birth", but it can't go on like that forever.

We need infrastructure for volunteers and researchers, but we need money to pay for materials and salaries. We need to educate the population; this is a fundamental requirement for conservation. Without the awareness of the inhabitants, there is no way to protect nature. We need resources to go to the schools and seek out the participation of children and young people in the process, since they are the best messengers of any community. We must hire buses to bring them to the Reserve, so they can see with their own eyes what they must defend; so they can get to know the wildlife on which their own lives largely depend. We must offer them a little snack before they leave, that is such a beautiful custom here. Nobody leaves without having eaten something for the road, as they say, even if the snack is just some simple tortillas and a fruit drink.

Joaquín is very committed. He only speaks Spanish, but he is going anyways. He says that he will find someone there who speaks Spanish and make himself understood, in one way or another, if they are willing to understand. He knows every tree, every bush, and every corner of the reserve. He knows the secret lives of the animals, and no one can describe them more passionately.

He came to tell me his plans and who he plans to visit in Holland, Denmark and Sweden. He met a Dutch girl named Claudine, here in Cabo Blanco, and when she returned to Holland she contacted the Nephentes Conservationists Foundation. They are the ones organizing Joaquín's trip and he is very excited to go. I have a close fellowship with Joaquín, we share the same spirit and unique drive. We don't need to talk to know what we think about wildlife, we know just by looking at each other. It is a different symbiosis than the one we shared, because Joaquín and I are not a couple, but it is a symbiosis all the same.

He is going to stay at the home of a certain Tommy Åsberg in Stockholm, who is a teacher there. They met through a couple of Swedish researchers who work in Turrialba. Can you imagine Joaquín, with his indigenous features, in Stockholm? Well, you can't imagine it, but I can't help but think of the astonished faces that people will have. Especially when he describes how jaguars and rattlesnakes live, while beaming with enthusiasm, and the organization and hierarchy of the Mantled Howler, White-faced Capuchin, and White-nosed Coati societies.

This trip and the correspondence with different associations, has reminded me of our struggle to buy the land for the reserve. I keep all the letters you sent and the responses, and I check them from time to time, to make sure that they are still there, as reliable witnesses, the guardians of the course of events. Also, because perhaps one day the letters will help to tell the history of the Reserve and leave a legacy for the people of Cabo Blanco. Only they can defend wildlife from the destructive fury of those who are fleetingly passing through, or those who want to get rich by stealing the habitat of other beings. Before any other consideration they must understand that their life depends on the life of the Reserve.

Joaquín has returned and he is very satisfied. He described a project negotiated with a Danish construction company that regularly donates to and collaborates with Nephentes. The agreement is to build a laboratory in San Miguel and a Ranger Station in Cabuya. They will bring prefabricated buildings and two teams of specialized Danish carpenters to assemble them during the two-week summer vacation. I am amazed and pleased by the generosity of my countrymen. Although I don't like the idea of building in the reserve, I know that a place is needed for research and to house students and volunteers.

It must be a minimal structure which causes minimal interference to the wildlife of the reserve. Joaquín is the best guarantee that this will be the case, of course, as long as he is here, spoiling his child; our child.

A Swede in Cabo Blanco

1991

*D*ear Olof, today I heard a language again that is so near to my memory. Tommy Åsberg, the Swede who hosted Joaquín on his trip to Scandinavia last year, has arrived. One of the actions they took together then was to visit the office of the Swedish International Development Cooperation. There they proposed the creation of a commission to contribute to the improvement and maintenance of the Reserve.

He showed me videos from different schools in Copenhagen. Hours of recordings, as Joaquín explained each slide to the astonished children. They made a good team.

Tommy brought his camera and is constantly recording. He is so happy, chasing Joaquin through the forest and on the beach. His intentions to help Cabo Blanco can be very beneficial and they come at a critical time, to consolidate the protection of the Reserve. Among other ideas, he wants to create an association for the Reserve. This way, the donations that he hopes to receive can be channeled through a series of activities geared to raise awareness in Sweden. They will be aimed at his students and conservation associations.

We both believe in the importance of environmental education for children and he has a project in mind for the schools here. A transversal student exchange program between both countries.

Imagine what it will be like for the kids on both sides to experience something so different from their normal lives.

Yes, I think it is essential to raise awareness on both sides. It is not easy for the kids from here to get out and learn about other regions, even in their own country. Sometimes, when we talk about that which is our own to someone who does not know it, we gain a better understanding of it. It is a way of nurturing our identity as individuals and as a society.

Tommy is a teacher at the Hässelby Villastads Skola educational center, located northwest of Stockholm. He is going to make the proposal to the school administration and to the parents of the students. The idea is to collect money by different means, with the intention of creating an environmental education program in the schools of the towns near the Cabo Blanco Reserve. He has assured me it will succeed, because Joaquín's visit has left a deep impression on all the teachers and students who met him.

This is all due to Joaquín's good work. No one can be indifferent to his passion and tenderness with nature. Tommy said that his students listened to Joaquín talk about the history of the reserve with emotion throbbing in their young eyes, amazed by what he showed them. They didn't even blink as he spoke, although they did not understand him and they had to wait for him to finish speaking to hear the translation.

Joaquín let me know that they finally approved the creation of the Association of Friends of Cabo Blanco. This news fills me with joy. Not only because of what it means economically, but because through the association your countrymen will get to know what we have created and learn to value it. It is a rewarding form of recognition and an injection of encouragement to continue. Sometimes recognition is more important than money.

I'm going to tell you something that happened two days ago. There is an English boy, Ray, who has lived in our house in Cocalito for almost a month. He is a young man who does not have many resources. I let him live in Cocalito for a few months in exchange for him helping me maintain order and watching over the place while I attend to the cabins.

A yellow tabby cat came to the house almost six months ago and stayed. It turned out she was pregnant and two weeks ago she had three beautiful, multicolored kittens. She created a comfortable place for them under the bed, on an old sheet.

Ray went to look for them yesterday and he couldn't find the kittens or the mother, but there was the boa under the bed. He pulled the sheet out from under the bed, dragging the boa, which had swallowed the kittens along with part of the sheet. Three well-defined lumps could be seen in her body.

He did not know what to do. He came running to Montezuma to tell me about it, but I told him it wasn't the first time it had happened. I told him what had happened to *Lis'* litter and he calmed down and returned to Cocalito. The cat did not return, but I imagine that she will be back when she overcomes her fear.

***

Finally and blissfully, the rains have arrived. The rain has superseded its quota this October, so I haven't been able to go up to visit you. The curtains of torrential rain blew in like a waterspout from the sea and it seemed that they would never stop. The leaves of the trees are constantly soaked and the branches bend under the weight of the water. There is half a meter of mud on the road, and Playa Colorada stream is raging, like the day you couldn't cross it. It is impossible to go outside, in the morning or in the afternoon, so I spend most of my time talking to the few visitors who come to the house and to my cats, especially with *Mis-mis*. Fortunately, I have enough batteries for the turntable. Listening to music during these days of forced confinement is a balm for the body and soul. Mahler is a very inspiring companion, even if he is sometimes tragic. It depends on my mood each day. If the day is not right for Mahler, I turn to Joaquín Rodrigo; you know my weakness for The Aranjuez concert. If I need more encouragement, there's The Nutcracker, which reminds me of the girl I used to be, dancing on the balls of my feet. Even *Lis* stands still if she arrives when Tchaikovsky is playing. I am convinced that without music, the world would be a less inhabitable and hospitable place.

1992

I am horrified, Olof, and furious about a development being built by a Spanish group in Tambor Bay. They will cause unprecedented environmental destruction, from the looks of it, perhaps the worst in the country's history. As Tommy Åsberg tells me, indignantly, they are destroying and razing the natural mangrove and the dunes to build a golf course and a hotel. The destruction of several hectares of wetland, which is home to countless wonderful creatures with the same right to life that we have, to sow a field that will lack the necessary water to maintain it.

Imagine, in a place where potable water is scarce and service for domestic use is restricted during the summer. They cut down the trees that hinder their development already and have committed who knows how many other environmental atrocities. All under the protection of politicians, with the promise of work for the population. But everyone knows that qualified jobs are filled with employees that they bring from Spain. The poorest quality and poorly paid jobs are left to the locals, under the guise that they are not qualified. Perhaps that is the case, which is why they should concentrate on improving the schools, so that the population is part of a development project that benefits them. If this is not the case, it simply causes a greater social and economic gap.

Tell me: is visiting natural areas to appreciate their beauty without disturbing wildlife even possible? Where will that brand of tourism be when there is no more life to observe?

The maritime-terrestrial zone will also be affected, because all the species born in the mangrove take refuge there until they are large enough to survive in the waters of the gulf. If water from the rivers does not flow into the ocean life will be altered and will not evolve at its natural pace.

Our neighbor John, as well as Luis and other people from the Conservationist Association, are fighting with all the means at their disposal and continually denounce the aggressions wrought upon the land. None of his complaints have succeed, however, and they have been branded as conservationist hippies, as if that were a crime. The Minister of Tourism even called Luis a traitor to the country.

My trip to Denmark

Dear Olof, I will travel to Denmark on May 18 with Álvaro Ugalde and Joaquín. I have no desire to return after so many years have passed and so many changes in my life and I suppose even more changes in my country. But Joaquín and Álvaro have insisted that I accompany them. They say that it is me they want to see and to hear the story from my own mouth; that they won't accomplish as much if I don't go.

It is a bit of emotional blackmail, but finally I have accepted, because we need the help that the Danish Government offers us to protect the Reserve. It will be a short and bumpy trip. This is our schedule: on the 21st, we will be in Odense, on the 22nd in Kolding, 23rd in Holstebro and there I will try to see my sister. I don't know if it will be a good idea, after so many years have passed, but I can always change my mind when I get there. On the 24th and 25th we will be in Aarhus and the rest of the days, until the 29th, in Copenhagen. We will return on the 30th, probably exhausted. I hope at least I can keep warm. They have chosen the right season; May is a beautiful month in Europe, with long sunny days. Surely, I will have many things to tell you upon my return.

My love, coming home is like being born again. I arrived three days ago, tired and happy to breathe this longed-for air. The rains have come while I was in Denmark and everything is green and beautiful, brand new. My cats have grown and multiplied. I have three new babies. A cat with four kittens has also arrived in Cocalito. While I would prefer not to have domestic animals there, I can't help but let them stay. This trip has made me think that no matter what happens, I will never leave here again. And if I stay, there is no reason the cats should not be allowed to stay as well.

I don't even know where to begin describing the trip. Copenhagen has changed so much, as well as the other cities. In Holstebro, I couldn't recognize the streets and where they led no matter how hard I tried. Luckily, I didn't have to look for my old house.

Everything is unrecognizable, except for the old official buildings, the result of so-called progress. I did not have time to walk the streets because the representative of Nepenthes, Mogens Siegerdahl, had everything organized: lodging and the conferences in the associations, high schools, and universities.

I must admit it was exciting to talk to them about everything we lived together while they listened avidly. The conferences had a single format. Mogens began by introducing us. Then it was me who explained the story you already know. Our story. Álvaro continued with the talk detailing Costa Rica's National Parks System. Then Joaquín briefly talked about the flora and fauna of Cabo Blanco. As Álvaro said, he didn't need to say a word, his role was fulfilled by his presence, with his indigenous features and his chest full of trinkets that hung from his neck.

When we were at the airport, waiting to board, Álvaro analyzed our trip and came to the conclusion that we were like a team of comedians. I was the saint who saved the world from my home in Costa Rica. Joaquín was the savior of wild animals. Álvaro was the ringmaster. His father, who accompanied us on this trip, was the one in charge of passing around the hat for the collection. We laughed so much with this parody; it was the only truly funny moment.

There were television and newspapers interviews after each presentation, and we were exhausted when we returned to our lodging. We were housed by families that collaborate in the Nephentes projects, each of us in a different house.

My sister Lis was the only family member that I saw. Thankfully, she came to the talk at the University of Holstebro and we met afterwards. We were both very excited. If the meeting had been before the talk, I might not have been able to address the audience. We spent three hours remembering things from our childhood. I told her that I named a coati after her and she laughed heartily. We both realized how much we miss each other and how we have suffered with the separation. Each person's life is unique, though, and everyone follows their own path.

We look very much alike, even more now that we are old than when we were young.

I relived the days of seventeen hours of light. The first day I liked it, but after that it was exhausting. The days never end so we can go rest. You can't regulate yourself by sunlight and you need to look at the clock to know what to do. I missed my cats and my pochote trees. One day when I was sitting in the park, before entering the lecture at a school, I cut some leaves from a tree and chewed on them. Álvaro gave me a disapproving look, as if I were a child. He told me they could be contaminated, that I was risking intoxication and I should not think that those trees were in the same condition as those of Montezuma. I could only smile at him, moved by his concern.

I feel so happy to be home again. I believe that life has been generous to us, despite what we have suffered here, especially with me. It has allowed me to live a fabulous life that I would never have dared to dream of.

Karen Mogensen y Álvaro Ugalde 1992 en Copenhague.

The Chorotega Corridor

*I'*m worried about something that Joaquín told me today about a property that they are selling near the Reserve. The land belongs to Doña Carmen Álvarez and National Parks have contested it, but the institution does not have the money for the purchase. Now Rolando, Camilo's son, is buying the land. For the past year Mrs. Carmen has been making arrangements for the National Parks System to release the land for sale and the paperwork for the property titles is complete. Soon the sale will go through because the woman, who is a widow, needs the money to live. If Rolando doesn't buy it, she will sell it to others who may be less considerate when the money is finally available in National Parks. In other words, Rolando's purchase may not be the worst alternative. But we cannot ignore the fact that the animals will have less space with the sale, although they do not understand borders.

Joaquín asked John if he could buy the land and donate it to the reserve, but John said that he has already donated a lot of money and he will not give more. And yes, it's true, thanks to John a lot of land has been purchased to expand the reserve. But we feel that every nearby land sale is a threat to wildlife. Who knows what the new owners will do, maybe sell it again. I also understand that this woman needs the money, but it is terrible that the Government cannot dispose of fifteen-thousand Dollars, which is the sale price. Anyway, it seems that this time we have no alternatives, although Joaquín has been trying.

Olof, I have some good news, although with a bit of a nasty side. John has finally decided to buy the land and donate it to Cabo Blanco. He couldn't resist the pressure from Joaquín, who was relentless until the end. The unpleasant part is that Rolando is very angry because of the way the purchase was made, and he is right. Rolando has been John's trusted employee for almost twenty years and had told his employer that the farm was for sale. Apparently, Donna told John to buy it and make the donation, but John had not wanted to.

Today, one year later, when all the parties were ready to sign for Rolando to buy the land at the National Parks offices in San José, John told Joaquín to call the National Parks and tell them not authorize the sale, because now he will buy the land and donate it.

So, I have mixed feelings. I am very happy, but at the same time worried. I know that Rolando is very angry with Joaquín because it was Joaquín himself who made the call to the director of National Parks. We had many shared experiences with Rolando, so I have great affection for him. When he was just a little boy, he was our postman for years and after you passed, he helped me when I needed him. But nothing is above the interests of Cabo Blanco, not even my life.

I know that Rolando is also angry with John and has told him that he is leaving. Donna told me all this. When John told her, she told her husband that she didn't want to see him for a week, so he grabbed a bag with four rags and took a hike. I don't think he will go beyond Puntarenas. John is like that, carefree and somewhat extravagant but also very generous. Without his help, Cabo Blanco would be smaller and more vulnerable.

I have some bad news, Olof, I am not at all happy. Joaquín has been reassigned to Cocos Island. It is hard for me to believe that he has accepted the post that Álvaro Ugalde offered him. Joaquín loves Cabo Blanco as much as we do, and he has shown his love every hour that he has spent in the reserve over the years. He came to tell me two days ago. He arrived with sorrow in his eyes, as if apologizing; but we can't blame him for anything. No one else could accomplish the colossal task that he was able to achieve here. None of our efforts would have been preserved if it weren't for his trips to Europe asking for help with the Reserve. The best thing is that the other park rangers love him. He is the first one to get to work, no matter how difficult the task, and he always risks the most when chasing off the hunters.

I asked him where the island was located, since I had never heard of it, and he showed me on the map. It is located between Colombia and Costa Rica and harbors legends of pirates and hidden treasures that no one has managed to find. After Costa Rica claimed the island, they turned it into a penal colony for political prisoners. Go figure!! That remote location. The human condition is miserable sometimes. Condemning someone for having different ideas is abominable. I prefer wild animals a thousand times, they are governed by their own instincts, without elaborating perfidious tortures against their adversaries. Perhaps because they recognize the difference between enemies and adversaries, better than humans do.

I don't know when they decided to protect it but sending Joaquín shows that there is a real commitment to conserving the island. He is the greatest conservation expert in this country, without question, and he was recognized as such in Europe. No one can be indifferent to his passion for wildlife, not even the frigid Europeans.

I visited the reserve yesterday and I was chatting with Stanley Arguedas, the new administrator. I'm not going to say that he's like Joaquín, because no two people are the same, and they have no physical resemblance. His eyes are as intensely blue as yours. It seemed to me that he could be a good successor to Joaquín, however. He has a very cordial attitude towards the entire team.

The tide was very low as I walked back to Montezuma, so I took the opportunity to cross over to Cabuya Island and visit the cemetery. It is a very original idea, even exotic, to make a cemetery on the island. It could emanate thousands of indigenous stories because they also used the island as a burial ground. It made me wonder why some were buried on the island and others on the mainland, because there are also several burials near the Reserve. People have found pots, necklaces and various objects that leave no doubt of their presence.

Julián, our neighbor from Montezuma, told me a legend long ago. He said that when there was an outbreak, those who contracted a plague were confined to that place, to avoid contagion. The ones who survived could return; the ones who didn't remained and in time the vermin took their corpse. He also told me about a ghost that appeared to a widow who had not fulfilled the rites of the dead.

I know very well that they really enjoy stories and legends around here, but I don't know if there is a real basis for it. The truth is that it is a place of peace and the tombs are neatly arranged, with beautiful promises of love and remembrance. They all have decorations made of shells and I can't help but wonder, if we keep stealing what belongs to the sea, how much more can we expect from it?

The cemetery is surrounded by almond trees that have become very large and leafy and that give the tombs a peaceful shade. I was careful with the time of return. Since the 1990 earthquake, when part of the bottom of the channel was raised, the window to cross the passage to the island before it is once again covered with water has narrowed. Although I don't notice any difference compared to the first time we visited, that day when we were surprised to observe four women carrying a small white coffin. They were dressed in white and their faces were devastated in tears. I remember thinking at that moment how unprepared we are to accept death. However, it is the only thing which is guaranteed to us when we are born. There is something ill-conceived in our culture that prevents us from accepting life in a continuous cycle, of which death is a part.

Years ago I read a story by Carmen Lira, a local writer, about the need for death to do its job, because otherwise, nothing could be renewed. Everything would grow old and nothing new could blossom. It is an interesting story that invites reflection. That teacher was graceful in describing the common, everyday occurrences of rural areas, in a natural and simple way.

Recognitions

1993

I have been made an Honorary Member of the National Park Service. It is a recognition of our work, but like all recognitions, it is an unnecessary honor. I would prefer another type of gesture. Something that truly demonstrates that the idea on which we created Cabo Blanco is backed by actions of conservation.

I still do not understand that inconsistency of the Minaet as an overseer of natural resources, energy, and mining. Isn't that deeply contradictory? How is the Ministry of Energy and Mining going to defend natural resources? It is perfect schizophrenia which is impossible in principle.

I got hold of a Science magazine at the Lehmann Bookstore on my last trip to San José. It contains a special section on recent research on the decrease of fauna in the forests. It addresses the issue broadly and accepts that human activity is accelerating the disappearance of many animal species, through the destruction of wild lands, the consumption of animals as resources or luxuries, and the persecution of species that humans perceive as threats or competitors in food consumption. But the authors of the article consider that the socioeconomic causes of this defaunation are difficult to understand.

We need many more of these articles in the fight for conservation. I am going to write them to congratulate them on their work. This special section highlights animals that disappear from the planet as well as the complications that arise when some people try to protect them. Unfortunately, these complications are all too well known to us.

I have also bought Wille Trejos' book: *Corcovado. Meditations of a biologist*. It's a treasure. It has a simple narration catalyzed by one who wishes to be understood and with the passion one who derives unlimited enjoyment from the observation of life. Its Introductory Chapter is entitled "In search of happiness" and it begins with a reflection on the satisfactions that people seek in their lives. He concludes that there are seven tendencies that lead us to this end. It is a book that should be in all educational centers. It evaluates life from the perspective of a greater whole, from which no one on this planet can escape; not even the smallest ant. It beautifully explains the flow of energy in nature.

It also deals with hunger and proposes a mathematical formula to eliminate it with grains. He stresses the importance of not dedicating land to livestock production. He also talks about our brain and how it works. All of this in such an entertaining way that you can't stop reading. It's hard for me to leave the book in the room and go about my duties, it is quite a find. I wish the days had more hours so I could read it and go back to it every time I feel its call. I am enthralled and feel a close kinship to this biologist.

We received another recognition, Olof. They must be reviewing everything they have not done in the entire history of this country and trying to compensate for it this year. In this case I like the recognition better, because it's for both of us. I'll have to get used to it. I just received the letter announcing that they are giving us an award for our contribution to the improvement of the quality of life, recognizing our work towards the conservation of the forests of this country. It is beautiful to see it written like this, in plural, *To Karen and Nicolás*.

The cycle of life and death

1994

I haven't felt well for a long time, although I hate to complain. My digestions are heavy, I have noticed abdominal inflammation and sometimes liver pain. I feel like energy is leaving my body some days and I don't feel like doing anything. The color of my skin is haggard and withered to the touch, with thousands of small wrinkles. Time does not pass lightly. I don't know how much more I have left before I meet you. I wait serenely for that moment, without any fear, on the contrary, with the acceptance of what I longed for.

Life had traced our passage through this world as the process planner that governs the cosmos has ordered, and I have learned to accept its instructions. At first, it was not easy to accept the role which has been assigned us in this theater drama to which we have been invited. It was acceptance that eventually made it possible for us to pour our energy into this universal project, rowing with the current of existence. It would have been useless to stubbornly fight it.

Of course, there were times when it was hard for me to accept the plans as they were designed. Particularly when it came to your untimely death, as stated by Don Emiliano, the guide who helped me find you. I feel that when I go, I will do so with my time spent and my work finished, but there is something I have to do with some urgency: choose who will take care of our farm. To whom do I leave the task that can guarantee its preservation and who will accept that commitment?

I have spoken with Amelia Arias several times, testing her, because she is younger and has continued the task that her husband Alejandro Pérez began in the Curú Reserve. Finally, a month ago I spoke to her directly, offering her our farm when I was no longer here. Her eyes widened and for a moment I didn't know if she was going to laugh or cry. She took me by the hand and told me that it was impossible for her to take care of anything other than Curú, since she had her hands full with all the work that the Reserve generated. In addition, she still had to take care of her children, who are very young.

She suggested I speak with the National Parks. She felt that it was an immense duty and responsibility, and that protection could only be guaranteed through a public institution.

Yes, I will speak with Álvaro Ugalde, once again. Although last time I spoke to him about my concerns for the future of my little forest, he shook his head in that emblematic gesture of his. He told me that I will never be able to decide, that it is too painful for me to make dispassionate decisions about the future. Perhaps I have voiced these concerns too many times before, without reaching a resolution and that makes him think I am incapable of deciding. I, however, believe that exploring different possibilities will finally allow me to choose the best option.

I have also thought about leaving it to Patricia and Lenny, as they're conservationists, but they're too involved in hotel development in the area and I'm not sure it's for the best. Also, they are educating their two children and I don't know if their education is focused towards business or conservationism. Is coexistence between the two even possible?

Allston Jenkins, president of the Philadelphia Conservationists, has written me a very cordial letter. I am going to ask for his opinion on this when I reply. Let's see what his advice is.

Patricia came over for breakfast today and she told me about a dream she last night. She was somewhat agitated and it is understandable: she dreamed that a large hotel had been built on our farm and that all the trees had been cut down. She envisioned lines of tourists coming and going with cars and asphalt roads, and a yacht marina at Playa Colorada. She explained it to me in full detail, as if she was seeing it in a movie. I listened to her in astonishment.

Her explanation was so painful at first that I didn't even want to finish listening to it. I went to a meeting in the reserve. But when I returned, after reflecting for several hours, I spoke with her again and decided that I can no longer delay the decision of making arrangements for the future of the farm. I want to meet with Joaquín, although he is already managing Cocos Island, but I am going to write him and ask him to come. I know he will heed my call.

Between the three of us we will make a list of the necessary conditions to make our farm an Absolute Reserve. It is the only way to guarantee the welfare of the animals that live there.

When Joaquín arrived he embraced me intensely, as if he wanted to transfer his energy to me. Then he looked at me serenely and asked how I felt. I did not want to expand on explanations about my health, because I feel bad, but I do not have a diagnosis. I asked him to find Patricia so we could get down to business with the farm. My decision to transfer it to National Parks was conditioned to making another absolute reserve: the Nicolás Wessberg. The three of us sat for hours, preparing a document on which to lay the foundations for protection. The activities that would not be allowed in the reserve were more important than those that what would be allowed, and this premise required careful detail.

I brought out the latest cadastral plans that I requested last year. It will be a year soon, they are dated September 2, 1993.

I felt so exhausted after Joaquín left that Patricia insisted that I should see a doctor to find out what is causing my pain and indigestion. She has set up an appointment with an internist recommended by a friend from Heredia. His name is Francisco Hera and he has a modern office. The walls are painted in pastel tones and there are European magazines in the waiting room with classical music playing in the background. Things have changed so much in this country.

He listened very carefully as I explained the symptoms in as much detail as I could. He immediately requested a complete blood test and an ultrasound test, after he examined the painful area with his hands.

We spent the night at Maria's house, Patricia's friend, and we returned the next day for the results. The doctor spoke only to Patricia, because he thought she was my daughter. After their conversation, she told me that she needed some time to assimilate before explaining the diagnosis. I respected her, although I thought that the diagnosis was mine and that it should have been delivered to me directly, but I did not want to contribute to her discomfort. She spoke to me after regaining her composure.

I have a very large tumor in the gallbladder which is invading the liver and causing biliary obstruction. An adenocarcinoma in advanced terminal stage and is not operable. I did not want to enter a hospital in San José. I don't know how long I have left to live, but I want to live in nature, not in a city hospital.

It is ironic, despite all my attempts to escape this terrible disease it has caught up with me. I think it could be worse, however. I saw it in one of the science magazines in the office. Neurodegenerative diseases, Alzheimer's for example. What an awful tragedy to stop being yourself, to forget who you are and the relationship you have with your family and the environment. I think that cancer, in my case, is not so terrible. Fortunately, the doctor has not proposed any treatment to alleviate the disease, except morphine when the pain is unbearable. I accept, once again, what life has in store for me.

I immediately called Álvaro to explain the situation. I asked him to go with the minister to the vicinity of the airport. I did not have the strength to go to San José and I needed to explain my conditions before naming the National Parks System as heir to our farm. I demanded, once again, for the same formula that we had in Cabo Blanco. An Absolute Reserve which would bear your name.

They arrived at the airport in an official car; Patricia and I were already there waiting in her car. The four of us met in the official car and we read the document written in Joaquín's handwriting right on the spot, as if it were a clandestine meeting.

They knew that they were talking to a dying woman and did not dare deny any of the demands in the document. We would make it official in a notary's office and the minister would have to sign it. I took advantage of my hopeless state to rigorously impose, without drama, the fulfillment of my conditions. I didn't have many alternatives, but they didn't know that.

We returned to Heredia to prepare the testament accepted by National Parks and to present it before a notary. We signed it today, September 6, at ten in the morning. It is a testament handwritten by the notary himself now in favor of the National Parks System and repeals my previous testament, which listed WWF and IUCN as heirs. The priority condition of this testament is the care and protection of the wild animals that live on the farm we own, which will be called the Nicolás Wessberg Absolute Reserve. After signing it, I went back to bed with a sense that my duty was fulfilled.

I drift towards you

I am fading, like a balloon that slowly deflates, loosing air imperceptibly. Patricia and Lenny brought me to their house and brought the bed outside under the trees with ocean view, so that I felt surrounded by nature. Although they do their best for me, sometimes I would like to stop breathing and finish once and for all to go be with you.

Nery came to visit this morning with a pile of tortillas she patted for me. I couldn't eat a whole one, but I was happy feeling the taste of the still warm corn on my lips.

September 9th

Olof, today they approved the Decree for the Declaration of Nicolás Wessberg Absolute Nature Reserve. Upon receiving the news, I feel energy returning to me for a moment. Once again we made it, my love. Your name will be eternally fused to our forest. I think all of the struggle, suffering, and these years without you by my side were worth it.

Now I just need to sign the power of attorney for Patricia, so that she can hand over the money I have left to the Cabo Blanco Administration to buy more land when I'm gone. I am dedicated to protecting Cabo Blanco until my very last breath.

September 25th

Dear Olof, a surprising letter has arrived today, now that my strength has diminished more than expected. It's from an American couple, Mike and Julie, who were here on vacation last February. In a long, detailed, letter they tell me about the events in their life since then, even how they are decorating the house for the arrival of their baby.

I put them up in Cocalito, in our cabin, and lent them the book *Living the Good Life*. While we were walking to Cocalito from Montezuma, they were telling me about their desire to have children, but all their attempts had been unsuccessful. As they were talking, I thought about other couples in the same situation. Couples who had tried to have children for years who managed to conceive after their stay here. In two cases they had already resigned themselves to starting the adoption process before they conceived.

The letter, written ten days ago, says that Julie is pregnant, and she originally had triplets. She lost one of them early on. A boy and a girl remained, but then she lost the girl. Now, they tell me that she is about to give birth to a boy and they will name him Nicholas. You see, the children that didn't come for us have turned the dreams of other families into reality. I am certain that all these couples conceived due to such intimate contact with nature, due to the incessant clamor of life. Fertility is in the environment and it is contagious. Where there is life, more life is begotten.

That is Cocalito, a seedbed of life. In the letter they invite me to go to their house to take a break from work, they say I can stay as long as I want. They have no idea that I am about to embark on a journey for which I do not need a ticket, but in another direction.

October 3rd

I have the feeling that today will be my last visit to Cóbano. I barely had enough strength to sign the transfer document of the little house in Montezuma over to Patricia in the municipality. I know I will not be here much longer, so one by one, I have sorted out my affairs. I would not want Patricia and her family to have problems with the property when I am not here. I can go in peace now.

When I returned, I went back to my bed, which was made up with immaculate sheets, and laid among the trees. Patricia and Lenny do the impossible every day to make me feel good, but my well-being no longer depends on them.

I called Syska and Moraya to come to my side, and they arrived with concern fanned out across their precious little faces. I wanted to be able to speak to them before my deterioration prevented it. Syska's eyes lit up when I told her that *Mis Mis* would be hers, then she blushed, as if she was ashamed of her joy. She loves cats and I think my favorite kitten will be happy with Syska. Moraya looked at me with a gravity that overcomes his eyes when something really worries him. They are as close to grandchildren as I would have liked to have and I have felt loved by them, as if they carried my family name. I remember what the fortune teller told me: "if you keep your eyes open, life will give you gifts." I always kept them wide open; and life was bountiful. A life intensely lived until the end.

I have been very happy here, in this land that gave me shelter and to which I have expressed my gratitude and respect each day. I feel privileged to reach this moment, a moment where I can't recognize what remains of the person I was. It feels natural to leave now that my task has been accomplished. I know that I am leaving an insecure and unjust world, but it no longer worries me, as I no longer have to face the troubles that afflict humanity. Others must take up the baton in the fight for life.

To them I give the words of my beloved Emily Dickinson:

"Hope is the thing with feathers, that perches in the soul..."

I am almost finished with this notebook filled with messages addressed to you, which are really addressed to myself, to help me carry on until now. Material evidence of continuity. It has been something solid to hold on to, at a time when everything was fragile and insecure. As volatile as bright ideas that hold so much promise and then turn out to be superfluous or simply erased from memory.

I ask Patricia a final favor: to accept the legacy of this notebook, which contains everything I have been writing since your disappearance, as well as the letters and photographs that we compiled since we left Sweden. I have also authorized her to publish it at some point if it would somehow serve the purpose of defending wildlife. I hope my journal finds someone with the same sensitivity and compassion for all living things. She has brought me a small tape recorder, which rests here beside me. To her I entrust this last soliloquy.

October 7th

It is 7 o'clock in the morning. Night slips around me and I have stopped fighting the pain; I don't feel it anymore. My body is abandoned, as in an expected *shavasana*. My organs stop working and they are shapeless in the structure of my body. They dissolve like electrical breakers, switched off one by one, and darkness slices through my tissues like a knife, relieving me of them. It doesn't scare me because I know that the night is darkest before dawn. I know, above all else, that I am heading towards you.

I already see you, advancing towards me with open arms, from the light of a tunnel that dazzles like your smile. I have waited so long for this moment that I tremble with happiness. I always thought death was going to be like this, like sliding down a bed of soft sand. Letting myself go effortlessly. All the effort is behind me, in a legacy fulfilled. I feel the energy of all my colleagues who helped me live without you fading. Some have left before me, with the dignity and manner borne by wild animals: at the bottom of their dens, stealing their privacy from the obscene gaze of others.

Give me your longing hand. You haven't aged my love, you're the same, wearing the same clothes that you left home with that day in July when you didn't return. Could it be that everything remains in this other world, that lies in the unknown? Ironically, I arrived battered by the illness that we fled from, it is she that brings me to you.

I have a thousand questions for you. They have been piling up because only I have been speaking all these years. But now you are my guide again, and this time it is forever. I will merge with you and nothing in this world or the next will pull me from your side.

Karen at Playa Colorada

Epilogue

Beyond death

*T*hose who accompanied her until her last breath know that Doña Karen departed the same way she had lived: with her dignity intact and with the discretion of wild animals. There were many who accompanied her on her last walk on the beach, that rainy afternoon on October 7, 1994. If they had been asked which feeling characterized this Madremonte, this Mother of the Forest, without a doubt they would all coincide in saying: love and compassion for all living beings.

It would possibly be the first time that the inhabitants of the Pueblos of Cabo Blanco would reach consensus. Although the chronicle of her death was announced, they would surely say that "Only death is reached too early", emulating Yolanda Oreamuno. In this case, too, the adage was true. Karen, however, thought that we were placed on this planet with our allotted time indicated by the cosmic order, and that the flow of time granted is finite. The only choice for each individual is how we manage that treasure that is our time here. That precious and limited time, like grains of sand that fall through an hourglass. It is our greatest wealth. Whoever dedicates their time to us, he gives us their greatest resource.

The funeral procession crossed the Playa Colorada, leaving their footprints in the sand. It was numerous and diverse. Park rangers, hoteliers, fishermen, farmers, children, and women who were there in their own right, paying the ultimate tribute to their loyal friend. They would always remember her with her white dress and her inviting smile, because she had taught them to relate in a new way; to be friends and confidants. To help each other in the trade of survival.

The procession stopped next to the Nicolás Wessberg Absolute National Reserve plaque, which was placed that same day, as a respectful gesture. At that moment, only some broken sobs and the coming and going of the sea could be heard. That's where the procession ended. The remainder of the journey with the coffin, up the mountain, would be undertaken by Doña Karen with her faithful squires, the Cabo Blanco park rangers: Joaquín, Stanley, Luís Mena and Carlos.

The whispered conversations, spoken in different languages, blended with the coming and going of the waves, caressing the beach as if singing a languid blues of farewell. Grief was drawn on their faces as they turned around and returned to their homes, covered by umbrellas that also wept meekly.

On the last stretch to her refuge, she was accompanied only by those who carried her coffin, made with boards that still smelled of sawdust, sawn that same morning by Romano Cruz. When they lifted the coffin, they remarked that the load was hardly more than the boards themselves. The last few weeks she had stopped eating solid food, and her consumed body resembled more the skeleton of a little bird when it was deposited in the coffin. Following medical advice, they decided to bury her the same day, given the possible decomposition of her corpse due to the physical deterioration and the heat.

It was a stormy night. Thunder and lightning traced a thousand paths in the firmament, as if they wanted to point the way for Madremonte to follow. The Mantled Howlers cried all night. They were long, hoarse howls, until the air completely vacated their lungs. They spoke to their Madremonte. They knew that the spirit of Karen and Nicolás would walk with them among their beloved trees, their home forever.

According to the locals of Mal País, Cabuya and Montezuma, a few adventurous people have had the joy of a prodigious encounter on full moon nights, when Selene draws the silver path on the skin of the Pacific. A guardian has been spotted near the confines of Cabo Blanco; nocturnal, jealous, and permanent. There is no doubt if his identity, his white, blond hair and white clothes made from wild cotton contrast with the forest cover. Nicolás is ever vigilant over his creation, the Cabo Blanco Absolute Reserve.

They also say that throughout the Playa Colorada forest, a petite woman dressed in white wearing a canvas hat that covers her gray hair, walks the Quebrada Colorada with the footsteps of an elfin creature, until she reaches Playa Colorada. A herd of White-nosed Coatis walk beside her, while the Mantled Howlers greet her by singing their most beautiful howl until the break of dawn. It does not happen every night, only on nights in which the moon slides her bridal train majestically over the reefs of Playa Colorada around four in the morning. Karen remains the guardian of the Nicolás Wessberg Absolute National Reserve, the reserve bearing the name of the love that conquered her life forever.

No one has ever seen them together, but those who knew and loved them know that they are only separated for a few full moon nights. Those, nights that require special care for the creatures; because it is on those beautiful nights when predators emerge from their lairs, attracted by the brightness of the moon. Empty thieves of light and life, lacking their own light.

Karen and Nicolás, the souls of Cabo Blanco, continue their mission, protecting all the creatures that inhabit the Reserve. They observe, constantly alert, unheeding to human laws, those laws printed with ink on paper. Other, more subtle, laws govern the spiritual planes hidden in the inner cosmos of consciousness. They know that the elements that make up our body are the same as those that once founded the universe. We are, therefore, children of the stars, beyond life...beyond death.

In February 1996, the Karen Mogensen Wildlife Reserve was created in Jicaral de Puntarenas, in honor of this great defender of life in its purest form. The reserve is possible due to the work carried out by Joaquín Alvarado along with the Nephentes organization, from Denmark, who made the donation for the first purchase of land. This was intended to expand the Protective Zone of the Nicoya Peninsula. Bearing in mind that a large number of the rivers that irrigate the Nicoya Peninsula originate on the lands of the reserve. We can rest assured that, once again, Doña Karen continues to protect the cradle of life.

Chronology

1919

July 15th: Nils Olof Wessberg is born in Eberswalde-Branderburg, West Germany. His parents were Hugo Wessberg (Swedish) and Gertrude Geissler (German). They met and married in Germany and moved to Eskara, Sweden after Hugo finished his Forest Engineering studies.

1926

August 4th: Karen Mogensen is born in Mabjerg-Holstebro, Denmark. Her parents were Valdemar Mogensen and Christine Fischer. Her mother passed away and her father remarried. He owned a pulp mill for making paper in Holstebro.

1952

Nicolás and Karen meet at Humlegården Raw Food Guest House, Copenhagen, Denmark. They were married that same year.

1954

February 13th: Nicolás and Karen left Sweden on board the *Astrid Bakke*. They traveled through Central America, Mexico and California.

1955

May 15th: Nicolás and Karen arrive in Costa Rica. They settle in Montezuma and purchase a piece of land.

1960

Nicolás discovers remnants of primary forest in Cabo Blanco and begins writing letters requesting help to purchase the land from squatters.

1963

October 21st: Cabo Blanco Absolute Reserve is established.

1972

Carlos Castrillo, twenty-one years old, is hired as a park ranger in the Reserve and remains in that position until he retires.

1975

July 23rd: Nicolás is assassinated during his visit to Corcovado, on the Osa Peninsula.

1977

Karen relocated to Puntarenas. She teaches English and yoga classes to earn a living and pay land taxes.

1979

Karen returns to Montezuma and opens a hostel.

1980

Patricia Slump settles in Montezuma and becomes Karen's best friend.

1985

Joaquín Alvarado assumes the position of administrator of the Cabo Blanco Nature Reserve.

1990

Karen is interviewed in May by Danish television Channel 2,.

July and August: Eva Tellow, Nicolás's niece, visits Montezuma.

November: Joaquín Alvarado travels to Stockholm to raise funds for the expansion of the Cabo Blanco Reserve. He stays at Tommy Åsberg's home.

1991

Tommy Asberg travels to Costa Rica and founds the Friends of Cabo Blanco Association.

1992

May: Karen, Joaquín and Álvaro Ugalde travel to Denmark.

July: Joaquín Alvarado is appointed director of Cocos Island.

1993

May: Karen is made an honorary member of the National Park Service.

October: Karen and Nicolás receive the prize for the Improvement of the Quality of Life for their contribution to the conservation of the forests. Nicolás would receive his award posthumously.

1994

June: Karen's interview with María Isabel Casas.

September 2nd: Karen is diagnosed with liver cancer.

September 9th: The Nicolás Wessberg Absolute Nature Reserve is created

October 7th: Karen dies from liver cancer. Her funeral is attended by the entire town of Montezuma, as well as the President of the Republic José María Figueres Olsen and the first lady. Karen's body is taken by park rangers and buried next to Nicolás on their farm, with special permission from the Government.

1995

February 5th: Karen Mogensen Reserve is created

2015

January 10th: author's interview with Álvaro Ugalde while preparing to write the book.

February 14th: Álvaro Ugalde, founder and great defender of National Parks in Costa Rica, dies.

A LETTER FROM A HORSE

The other day I received a letter from an old horse. He was sick, ruined, and miserable, roaming the road between Cóbano and Moctezuma, on the Nicoya Peninsula.

Of course, he did not write it himself, as he does not have a hand to accomplish such a feat. This poor, martyrized horse, one of thousands of horses in Costa Rica, dictated the letter to a man who could interpret his language so he could transcribe it. This is what the horse said:

I have grown old working for the benefit of men. I briefly enjoyed freedom when I was young. I could roll around in the grass, run freely, and lay down at will. But soon I began to work for a man, and later other men. Rather than training me through gentle patience, they beat me, whipped me, and stabbed me with their spurs because I did not perform a task they demanded; a task that they had not bothered to teach me. Many times, they beat me on the neck and even on the head and one day when hitting me they took out my eye. Only brutish, stupid men behave this way. Many of my brethren have lost an eye enduring such abuse from brutish riders.

Other times they did not feed me. They tied me to a post when they did not need me and would not allow me to graze. Of course, they did not offer me a drink of water or a handful of corn or plantains to eat!

One of my owners would put dirty saddle pads on me that he never washed. They were full of holes and knots which rubbed my hide raw.

On many occasions they left me tied up under the hot sun for hours while they refreshed themselves in the shade, drinking beer, and who knows what else. They didn't even bother to loosen the hard muzzle and now I have lost sensitivity in my nose. In the rainy season I was left to spend the night in places where my hooves sank in the mud, so now my hooves are split and deformed, and I can hardly walk. They say a spider was to blame for the problems in my hooves, but that's a lie, it is the fault of man.

Many times I was limping and the brutal man riding on my back did not dismount to slowly lead me home, as a Christian, civilized and intelligent man might do. Instead, he made me carry him while he beat me, cursed at me, and spurred me. This abuse caused desmitis and I have chronic swelling in my knee, so now I am useless. Yet this Christian man claims that I was to blame for my condition.

When I was young, strong, and beautiful my owner would dress me up with fancy accessories and mount me to impress his neighbors. Then he sold me to another man who treated me badly, then that man sold me to another who treated me worse. When nobody would pay money for me, this last one gave me away to a poor man who did not provide for me because I "was worthless." When he wasn't beating me and forcing me to work, I was penned up in a corral with no food suited for a horse. There were only spines, Ironweed, Jelly Ear, and other weeds which, according to the man, should provide nourishment for a horse.

Finally, when he could not get me to work, even with the harshest tortures, this Christian man left me out to die in the street saying: "This horse is totally worthless."

So here I am: blind in my right eye, deaf in both ears, with swollen ligaments in my knee, sores on my back, my front hooves are split, broken and rotten, and I have thousands of ticks everywhere!

I know that the maggots crawling in my ears will kill me, but I will not have the quick death that we all wish for. So, I plead to those who own a horse or any other beast, I beg of you to do one last favor for your faithful workers: When your animals are old, don't sell them or give them away to any random person and don't abandon them in the streets. Please, put them out of their misery humanely, without pain or fear. If you don't do it yourself, make sure it is done correctly. Liberating an animal from a life of suffering is a humane act of compassion! Make sure there is no fear or pain in their final moments and that the end comes quickly! Thank you!

World Horse Protection League, London England

Olof Wessberg, Moctezuma

Puntarenas, Costa Rica

Acknowledgements

I want to acknowledge the people who have in one way or another made my life in Costa Rica possible and all those people who contributed to the telling of this story. I sincerely hope you feel recognized: Tommy Åsberg, Jaime García, Patricia Alpízar, Álvaro Ugalde, Carlos Castrillo, Julieta Valle de Shutt, Isidro Murillo, Rodrigo Soto, Patricia Slump, Nery Vargas, Romano Cruz, Man León, Frank Cortés, Mario Boza, Mitzy Spesny, Anacristina Rossi and Guillermo Lahtrop, Ana Burgaña, Georgina Botazzi, Pilar Saavedra, Angélica Zeledón and the Santa Teresa Rural School.

My infinite thanks to Martina Wegener and Gianfranco Gómez Zamora for the immense effort they have dedicated to this book.

About the author

Lola Pereira Varela, Spanish author, environmentalist and teacher through the Narrative of tales of the Oral Tradition. She is a specialist in Applied Emotional Intelligence and a Yoga teacher.

She lived in Costa Rica for 24 years, actively promoting reading and environmental awareness for the Ministry of Public Education. She is a co-founder of the Santa Teresa de Cóbano Rural Lyceum and host of the Santa Teresa Cultural Identity Rescue Program.

Her previous publications include *La Escuela del Mar* (2013) and *Recetas de Cuento* (2014). She was the winner of the call for Artistic Experiences, Culture and Citizenship from the Ministry of Public Education, the Ministry of Culture and Youth and the OEI, in 2009.

Index

Prologue 9

Part One

Harrowing dreams..………………………… 13

I search for you…...……………………........ 20

Where are you?....................................... 29

Reminiscing... 40

Aboard the Astrid Bakke.......................... 44

The New World……................................. 49

Costa Rica 58

Cabo Blanco... 67

I find you….. 77

The killer is captured............................... 85

Your funeral... 90

The trial and sentencing.......................... 94

Part Two

Never forget.. 105
The memory of ghosts....................... 110
The letters... 115
Lis... 126
Images and memories....................... 135
Puntarenas.. 143
English and Yoga classes................. 151
Your voyage to Punta Llorona......... 163
Cabinas Karen.................................. 168
A Dutch woman in Montezuma...... 177
A baby in the family........................ 189
Joaquín Alvarado............................. 199

Part Three

El Sano Banano................................ 212

The television... 223

A visit from Eva Tellow... 234

A Costa Rican in Sweden……….......................... 241

A Swede in Cabo Blanco.. 244

My trip to Denmark.. 250

The Chorotega Corridor... 255

Recognitions... 261

The cycle of life and death...................................... 264

I drift towards you.. 271

Epilogue

Beyond death.. 280

Chronology... 285

A Letter from a Horse.. 291

Acknowledgements.. 293

About the author.. 294

Lightning Source UK Ltd.
Milton Keynes UK
UKHW040721060323
418105UK00002B/342